'Brilliant, laugh-out-loud funny and **genuinely moving**'
M.G. Leonard, author of *Beetle Boy*

'**Full of heart** and **humour**, wit and wisdom'
Sophie Anderson, author of
The House With Chicken Legs

'**So good** you'll CLUCK with laughter!'
Pamela Butchart, author of
Baby Aliens Got My Teacher!

'Wonderfully **heart-warming** and **absolutely hilarious**'
Catherine Doyle, author of
The Storm Keeper's Island

'**Will have readers snorting with giggles**'
Northern Echo

'A **gloriously fun,** madcap adventure with a **celebration of friendship** at its heart.'
Anna James, author of *Pages & Co:
Tilly and the Bookwanderers*

'**Hysterically funny!**'
Jeremy Strong

Dear Luca,

Hope you enjoy!!

Sam Copeland is from Manchester and now lives in London with two smelly cats, three smelly children and one relatively clean-smelling wife. He works as a chicken whisperer, travelling the world using his unique gift to tame wild chickens. *Charlie Changes Into a Chicken* is his first book. He has threatened to write more.

Follow Sam online
@stubbleagent
#CharlieChangesIntoAChicken

SAM COPELAND

CHARLIE

CHANGES INTO A

CHICKEN

ILLUSTRATED BY
SARAH HORNE.

PUFFIN

PENGUIN BOOKS

UK | USA | Canada | Ireland | Australia
India | New Zealand | South Africa

Penguin Books is part of the Penguin Random House group of companies
whose addresses can be found at global.penguinrandomhouse.com.

www.penguin.co.uk
www.puffin.co.uk
www.ladybird.co.uk

Penguin
Random House
UK

First published 2019

008

Text copyright © Sam Copeland, 2019
Illustrations copyright © Sarah Horne, 2019

The moral right of the author and illustrator has been asserted

Text design by Janene Spencer
Printed in Great Britain by Clays Ltd, Elcograf S.p.A.

A CIP catalogue record for this book is available from the British Library

ISBN: 978–0–241–34621–1

All correspondence to
Penguin Books
Penguin Random House Children's
80 Strand, London WC2R ORL

For my father, Steve, who taught me
how to laugh in the toughest times

CHAPTER 1

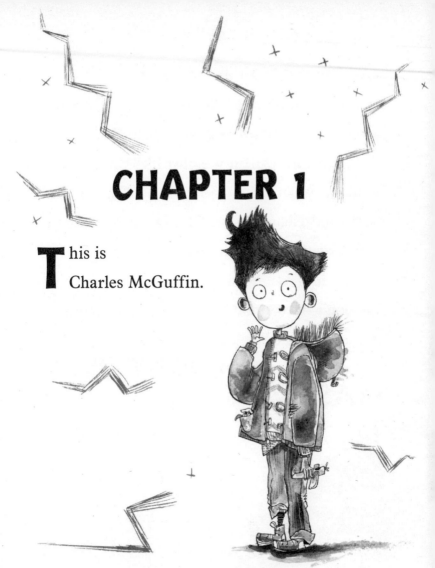

This is
Charles McGuffin.

It isn't *actually* him. It's just a picture of him.
OF COURSE. If you hadn't figured that out, this
book will be way too difficult for you and you

should probably go and read *The Really Simple Book of Dead Easy Stories for Total Numptyheads* instead.

Charles McGuffin was just like you and me. Well, he wasn't like me because I'm big and hairy, and Charles is small and pretty smooth. So he's just like you. Except he has a you-know-what, and I'm guessing many of you reading this don't have a you-know-what. So Charles is like *some* of you.

Except for one **MAJORLY HUGE, MASSIVE** difference.

He can change into animals.

As in, one minute he's a normal boy, the next minute he's a wolf.

Or an armadillo.

Or a danger noodle (which, as everyone knows, is the actual scientific name for a snake).

OK, so that probably means Charles is absolutely *nothing* like any of you because nobody else can change into animals.

I think it's probably best if we start this book again, don't you?

Just pretend you didn't read this bit, OK?

CHAPTER 1 (AGAIN)

CRRR...

This is Charles McGuffin.

It isn't *actually* him. It's just a picture of him. **OF COURSE.**

4

Charles McGuffin is absolutely nothing like you or me. He is totally, completely different. Charles is *unique*. Because Charles can transform into animals. Like danger noodles.

Now, Charlie[1] was a pretty normal boy until about three weeks after his ninth birthday. He'd just come back from visiting his older brother, SmoothMove, at the hospital for the zillionth time. SmoothMove was quite ill and had been in hospital for ages and ages. This was really annoying because Charlie was convinced he could now beat his brother at *FIFA* on the PS4 and wanted to prove it. Also, the den in the garden needed mending and Charlie couldn't do

[1] Although he's called Charles, everybody calls him Charlie for short, which is pretty silly because Charlie actually has the same number of letters as Charles.

P.S. This is called a footnote. It's called a footnote because when a clever person from ancient Greece thought of something really important and absolutely had to write it down so they didn't forget it, but didn't have any paper to write it on, they used to write it on their foot.

You know what, I'm not too sure about that fact. Don't trust me on that one.

it by himself. And sometimes Charlie just wanted his brother back so he had someone to play hide-and-seek with. Playing hide-and-seek by yourself isn't much fun – Charlie had tried.

If you're very clever, you might have guessed that Charlie's brother isn't *actually* called SmoothMove, but woe betide[2] you if you were to call him anything else. Charlie's brother's actual name was Henry, but after a lifetime of being called Horrid Henry he would punch anybody right on the nose if they called him by his real name. He was twelve years old, sick of hospital and could still easily beat Charlie at *FIFA*, no matter what Charlie said. And he might have a girlfriend, but he would punch you on the nose if you said, 'SmoothMove has a girlfriend.' In fact, you'd do well to come away

[2] Well spotted! It's another footnote. You're probably wondering what 'woe betide' means. Well, only parents and teachers are allowed to say, 'Woe betide you . . .' It's the law. But, if you want some fun, next time a teacher or parent says, 'Woe betide you,' ask them what it means. What it means *exactly*. You will probably see steam coming out of their ears and you'll get into more trouble but it will be worth it.

from any conversation with Charlie's brother without getting punched on the nose for one reason or another.

As soon as Charlie and his mum and dad got home from visiting SmoothMove, Charlie ran straight upstairs to his bedroom. He dived into his bed, under his duvet, and tried not to think about the **'big scan'** that his brother had just been telling him about. After a while, he wiped his eyes and propped the duvet up with a tennis racquet to turn his bed into a tent. Once the tent was steady and stopped collapsing, he switched on his torch and began reading his favourite book. Charlie's favourite book was about volcanoes. It had pictures of massive explosions and orangey-red lava, and he liked to imagine he was escaping certain death by sliding down the volcano, surfing lava and dodging explosions.

The sound of his parents arguing downstairs

rumbled through the house, low like thunder. Charlie closed his book. He couldn't concentrate. Darkness had fallen outside, and the street light outside Charlie's window was making uncanny shadows on his bedroom wall. The silhouettes of the tree branches looked a little too much like long, clutching witches' fingers for Charlie's liking, so, quick as a flash, he sprang out of bed and pulled his curtains together.

It was there and then that it first happened.

It began with a twitching in his eye. Charlie froze to the spot, feeling his eyelid blink manically. His eye had twitched before, when he'd been tired, but this felt different somehow. It felt like somebody had just plugged him into a wall socket. The twitching spread to his other eye, and both eyes were blinking and twitching.

A feeling burst through the whole of his body, like he'd just been shot through an electrical wire, like *he* was the electricity. Every part of his body **FIZZED** and **HUMMED**. The fizzing and humming became stronger, until he felt he was on fire, but a fire inside a never-ending tube, squeezed and vibrating.

His skin felt extraordinary. Alive. He looked at his arm and, with some considerable alarm, saw that hair was sprouting out of every part of his skin.

Weirdly the room was growing larger too.

But no, Charlie realized, the room wasn't growing larger – it was him who was shrinking! Smaller and smaller he shrank, the room growing ever larger around him.

And his body – Charlie hardly dared look – his body was transforming. Completely. Extra legs were growing out of him (which is every bit as gross as you could imagine). And finally he felt new eyes emerging out of his head (which was possibly even grosser than the new legs).

Charlie recognized almost immediately that he was turning into a spider.

And how did Charlie know this?

He looked at the *evidence*:

EVIDENCE 1: Charlie was now tiny. Admittedly he hadn't been that huge before he changed, but he could see a dried apricot under his bed that he'd been saving for a rainy day, and he was now about the same size as the apricot. And normal nine-year-old boys usually aren't the size of dried apricots.

EVIDENCE 2: Charlie counted his legs and he

had eight of them, which is about six too many legs for a human, but just the right number for a spider.

EVIDENCE 3: He was completely covered in short brown hair. Now, being covered in hair didn't necessarily stop someone from being human – take Charlie's Uncle Pete, for instance. Uncle Pete had taken Charlie swimming once and

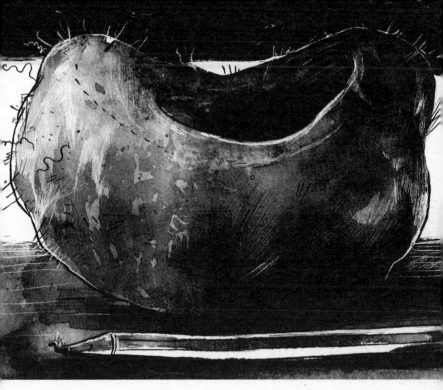

when he took off his T-shirt he had a back so covered in thick tufty hair a gorilla would have been jealous. All the other children had stopped and stared, wide-eyed and jaws agape, as Uncle Pete stepped into the pool, back hair fluttering in the breeze. Charlie had tried to forget this ever happened but the more he tried to forget Uncle Pete's Hairy Back, the more it stayed in his brain because brains are annoying like that.

EVIDENCE 4: Charlie was able to look nearly all the way behind himself, without even turning round. He reached up with one of his new, long, spindly black legs and carefully counted his eyes. There were eight.

Eight legs? Eight eyes? Veeery suspicious.

So Charlie looked at all the suspicious evidence and added small + hairy + eight spindly black legs + eight eyes together and got spider as the answer because it is a well-known fact that spiders are hairy and have eight legs and eight eyes. It's a less-known fact that spiders also have eight bums,[3] which is both disgusting and messy and also costs spiders loads of money in toilet roll.

Charlie sat on the floor and considered his

[3] If you are very clever, you will have realized that this is not actually a fact. It is actually completely untrue. Spiders only have one bum, for which they are very grateful. However, if everybody reading this can convince as many other people as they can that spiders DO have eight bums, then that would be awesome and the world would be a better place. So, if you have younger brothers and sisters, start by getting them to believe that spiders have eight bums.

predicament. He had turned into a spider and he had no idea how to spider. He'd had lots of practice being a boy, but zero practice spidering. After a short while just sitting there being a spider, Charlie came up with a plan. The plan had two simple steps. They were:

Step 1: PANIC!!!

Step 2: Shout to his mum to come and help.

He successfully carried out the first step of his plan. This mostly involved flapping his spindly legs in the air. After he'd panicked for an appropriate length of time, Charlie attempted to carry out Step 2.

Step 2 was unsuccessful. And why was Step 2 unsuccessful? Have you ever heard a spider shout? No. Of course you haven't. Because spiders can't shout. Spiders can't mutter, whisper, talk, chat, gossip, jibber-jabber or yodel in any way, and they definitely can't shout for help.

After a few seconds of silent shouting and

furious leg-waving, Spider-Charlie sat on the floor, next to the fluff-covered apricot, and realized that Step 2 of his plan was just not going to work. So he decided to go back and repeat Step 1.

CHAPTER 2

Now just snap out of it, Spider-Charlie, Charlie thought after a few minutes of spider-panicking. *There's no point in panicking. Things are going to get better, because they can't get any worse than they are right now.*

Charlie had never been more wrong about anything in his life.

Things were about to get a whole lot worse.

Any minute now, it will all be absolutely fine. Everything will be back to normal, Charlie thought to himself wrongishly.

You see, Charlie is what's known as an 'optimist'. That means he looks on the bright side of things, and always expects the best out of life. This is, ordinarily, the best way to be.

But perhaps being an optimist is not the best way to be when you have just changed into a spider. Then it's perhaps best if you become something of a 'pessimist'. A pessimist is the opposite of an optimist. Pessimists always expect the worst to happen such as:

1. My football team will lose four-nil and I will score four own goals.
2. I will absolutly fail my speling test on Friday.
3. After suddenly turning into a spider, things will not suddenly become better but, in fact, they will become much worse because the family cat, a big ginger tom called Chairman Meow, will come into the bedroom and try to eat me.

But Charlie was not a pessimist. He was an optimist. He was slowly calming down and panicking less because he was thinking positive thoughts.

This was a very bad idea, because edging through the bedroom doorway was a fat, furry ginger cat called Chairman Meow.

And Chairman Meow liked to eat spiders.

And Charlie was a spider.

You see where this is going? Finally so could Charlie. He froze in terror.

Chairman Meow's eyes glinted in the dark.

Charlie spider-gulped.

Chairman Meow lay flat, haunches in the air, ears pricked.

Charlie accidentally let out an eensy-weensy, teeny-weeny little terrified spider-fart.[4]

---

[4] Another footnote. I promise you, though, this one is interesting. Most animals do fart. Real scientists actually got paid actual money to make a list of animals that fart and animals that don't. That would be one seriously stinky laboratory. I bet they went home smelling of rhino farts and nobody wanted to stand next to them on the train. The scientists discovered that goats and baboons and whales (can you imagine that blast?) DO fart, whereas birds and crabs and oysters DON'T. And do you know what? Scientists don't know if spiders fart! Well, I think Charlie has just proved here conclusively that spiders DO fart. You can thank us later, Science.

Parp-pfft!

Chairman Meow wiggled his furry bum, getting ready to pounce.

Time seemed to **stretch** like a rubber band. Then it **snapped**. Charlie sprang into action. He skittered under his bed as fast as his eight legs could carry him.

Chairman Meow leaped after him.

Charlie ran as far and as fast as he could.

Chairman Meow couldn't quite reach Charlie, but began to swipe at him with his fat ginger paws. Charlie ducked and ran and jumped past the jabbing claws. He reached the corner of his room, under his bed, cowering among old lollipop sticks and dusty Match Attax cards, a rotten apple core and a dead snail that he'd kept as a pet until it had escaped and at least now he knew where it had ended up.

The swinging, swiping claws were getting nearer. Charlie had to think and think fast.

And then he realized – he would have to *spider* his way out of the situation. He put one spindly foot against the wall. And then another. And another. And another. And ano– Well, you get the idea. He placed all eight of his feet on the wall. And then he began walking. Up the wall.

Now this probably feels pretty normal to spiders, but Charlie did not feel it was in the least bit normal. Quite the opposite. In fact, as he climbed up the wall, Charlie would have been screaming at the top of his lungs, if spiders could scream (which as we already know they can't).

Spiders might not be able to scream, but they *are* able to see backwards, and this suddenly became a very useful, actual life-saving ability. Because Charlie saw behind him that Chairman Meow had spotted him. He could feel the cat thudding across the floor towards him through the vibrations in his spider-feet.

Charlie ran faster.

Chairman Meow pounced high, stretching to get Charlie.

He just missed. Charlie ran as fast as he could up to the top of the wall and on to the ceiling just above the wardrobe. He stood spider-still, upside down, utterly terrified, as Meow prowled menacingly below him.

Now this *is as bad as it gets*, thought Charlie. *It* can't *get any worse. It* definitely *has to get better from here.*

Charlie had still not learned his optimism/pessimism lesson.

In two swift, lithe leaps, Chairman Meow sprang first on to the bed, and then on to the top of the wardrobe. Without warning, Charlie was trapped upside down in the top corner of his bedroom, looking down at his pet cat, who was now inches away from eating him.

At no point had Charlie ever imagined that this would be how he would die: turned into a spider and then munched by a furry ginger cat. Life's funny like that.

This was it.

The end.

Game over.

And there would be no starting the level again.

The cat pounced, jaws wide.

Without knowing what he was doing Charlie jumped. And as he did, something weird shot out of one of his eight bums[5] and hit the ceiling behind him. A long silver rope.[6]

[5] Remember: eight bums. Keep the lie going. Let's make it happen.

[6] Technically spiders don't actually shoot webs out of their bums. They come out of tiny holes called 'spigots'. Spigots are actually a bit like tiny bumholes, but instead of poo they shoot out spider silk. Which is pretty awesome when you think about it. Now remember the word 'spigots', because one day in twenty-five years' time, it will be a crossword clue or a question in a quiz and everyone will think you are very clever for knowing it. 'Spigots' will also be a very useful word to know for a game called Scrabble.

24

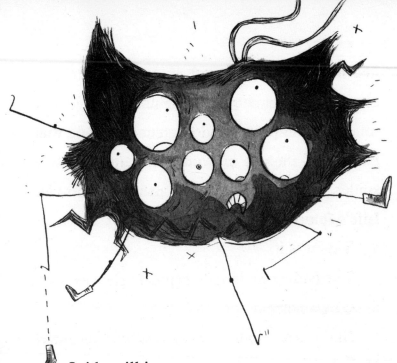

Spider silk!

Now, Charlie was only nine years old, but he knew – deep, deep down he just *knew*, with wisdom beyond his years – that this would be the single weirdest, freakiest, most loopy-freaky-bananas moment of his life.

And as Charlie soared through the air, swinging on his butt-rope, Chairman Meow watching wide-eyed and open-jawed, Charlie felt the electricity shoot through his body again, like he was being blasted up to a satellite and down into a mobile phone. He felt squashed and squeezed and pulled and stretched until he was huge, vast, the size of a boy again, and he could see his own legs back and his own arms, and he fell, fell and finally **KER-RASHED** on to his bed.

Charlie was no longer a spider. He was back to being a normal boy.

He lay there panting, staring at Chairman Meow, who still sat on top of the wardrobe, looking down at Charlie with as much disbelief as a cat can muster.

Charlie's bedroom door suddenly burst open. It was his mother, and she looked furious.

'**Charles McGuffin!** Do NOT jump on your bed! I have told you before: you will break it.'

'But, Mum –'

'Don't "but, Mum" me.

If you break it, then you'll have to sleep on the floor because we can't afford to buy you a new one. Honestly – it sounded like you were crashing through the ceiling.'

'But, Mum, I was a spider!'

'Spiders don't crash around like parachuting elephants.'

'But I changed back into me! Chairman Meow was about to eat me and I jumped out of the way and then when I was flying through the air I changed back into a boy and my bum-silk snapped and I crashed on to the bed.'

'Your bum-what? Actually, never mind. I don't want to know. Just, next time, try to land more gently. And, Chairman Meow – do not ever try to eat Charlie again.'

To be fair to Chairman Meow he did look a little shame-faced.

'You don't even believe me, do you? That I turned into a spider.' Charlie eyed his mum with a hurt expression. 'It wasn't just imagination, you know. It really happened.'

'Of course I believe you.'

She didn't. Charlie could tell by her voice and the little smile hiding at the corner of her mouth that she didn't really think he had actually turned into a spider but that he was just playing a game.

'Now, Spider-Man,' Charlie's mum continued, 'can you crawl downstairs for your dinner?'

Charlie couldn't help but smile back.

'Yeah. What is it?'

'Flies.'

Charlie's mum winked at him, and Charlie laughed, a lovely warm feeling spreading in his belly. He bolted down the stairs, only now realizing how starving hungry he was. Nearly getting eaten certainly gave you an appetite.

'And anyway,' Charlie's mum said as they sat down at the table, 'didn't you say you wanted to be a web designer when you're older?'

'Mum . . .'

CHAPTER 3

Charlie was walking down the school corridor with two of his three best friends, Mohsen and Wogan.

'You serious? You actually turned into a *spider*?' Mohsen said to Charlie, eyes wide.

'You believe me?' said Charlie with relief in his voice. 'My mum didn't.'

'Course she didn't. Adults never believe *anything*. That's what friends are for,' Mohsen said wisely.

Mohsen had a PS4 AND an X-box, but he had five sisters so that balanced out, Charlie thought.

Mohsen and Charlie had become best friends on their first day of reception when Charlie had been too shy to ask to go to the toilet and – well, you can guess what happened. You don't need it spelled out. It happens to everybody, OK? Even your mum or dad have had a little accident in their pants at one time or another. Go and ask them, if you don't believe me. Yes, right now. Go on. I'll wait.

. . .

. . .

. . .

I told you they had. And if they are reading this book out loud to you, have a look to see if they are blushing. If they are blushing, they definitely remember having an accident in their pants. And if they *aren't* blushing, they are probably not human and are almost certainly ROBOTS, in which case you need to check by tickling them. If they laugh, they are human, because robots aren't ticklish.

Anyway, back in reception, Mohsen had been kind and hadn't laughed at Charlie and had helped him to the toilet. Charlie had tears pricking at his eyes, but Mohsen had told him how he had pooed his own pants on the bus a few weeks earlier and the whole bus smelled of poo, and that made Charlie laugh and from that moment on they had been best friends.

'So you were like Spider-Man?' Wogan said, his eyes as wide as Mohsen's.

Wogan was the second of Charlie's best friends, and he was awesome at football but all the girls in his year kept trying to kiss him, so that balanced out, thought Charlie. Wogan was tall with unruly hair.

'No. Not at all,' Charlie replied. 'Spider-Man is a human with the powers of a spider because he got bitten by a radioactive spider. Spider-Man was as big as a human and looked like a human. I was the size of a spider and looked like a spider. I had eight legs. I wasn't Spider-Man. I was just . . .' Charlie thought for a moment. 'I was just . . . Spider, I suppose.'

The three boys pondered this as they approached their classroom.

'So, why did it happen, then?' Wogan asked. 'You know, Spider-Man got bitten by a spider, the Incredible Hulk got radioactivized, and Iron Man got hit on the head by an iron when he was a baby.'

'That's not how Iron Man became Iron Man, Wogan,' Mohsen said, shaking his head. 'I know what your brother told you but it's not true. Anyway, Iron Man doesn't count because he doesn't even have special powers like Charlie. He's just rich and puts on a robot suit.'

'I don't have special powers. It's just something that happened,' said Charlie glumly.

'Whatever,' Wogan said, waving his hand at Mohsen. 'It doesn't answer the question. Why *did* it happen, Charlie?'

'I don't know,' Charlie replied. 'But I need you guys to help me find out. And Flora too.'

'No. Not Flora. Please, no,' Mohsen and Wogan groaned.

Flora Fawner was Charlie's other best friend.

'She'll mess everything up. And she's scary,' Mohsen pleaded.

'She's not scary,' Charlie argued half-heartedly. 'She's . . . normal,' he added, uncertainly.

Wogan groaned again. 'Yeah, right. Sure.'

'Yeah, she's *totally* and *completely* one hundred per cent normal,' Mohsen scoffed.

'Well, she's our friend. And she's brave,' Charlie pointed out.

Mohsen and Wogan could not disagree with that. She was easily the bravest of the four of them. Last summer, a bee had flown in through the window of the shed they were all playing in. Charlie, Mohsen and Wogan had run out screaming. Flora, ice-cool, had picked up a cup and, calm as anything, trapped the bee against the window, picked up a piece of paper, slid it in between the window and the cup, and lifted the cup away with the bee trapped inside, walked slowly to the door, and let the bee out, off to bee freedom. The boys had stood staring at her in open-mouthed awe.

Yeeehaw!

Whenever there were bullies, Flora stepped in. Who had sorted it when some boys from the year above were taking Mohsen's snack bar every break? Flora. She hadn't done anything violent – she had merely sauntered up to the ringleader and whispered something in his ear. The boy had turned pale and immediately run away. He never bothered Mohsen again and they never did find out what she whispered in his ear.

Flora might be scary, but she was certainly brave. They needed Flora.

And as they walked into the classroom, there she was, sitting happily by herself. Today, she was wearing five different-coloured hairbands. Wedged in between the hairbands, poking their furry heads out, were some little toy trolls. Flora had dyed the hair of the little trolls black.

INTERLUDE

You might have noticed at this point that there has been no description of Charlie in this book. There are drawings of him in the book, but he doesn't ACTUALLY look like that. It's what's called an 'artist's impression'. That's somebody else's idea of what Charlie looks like. Maybe you think he looks totally different. Perhaps you have already imagined him in your head.

Close your eyes and try to imagine what Charlie looks like.

Actually that's a silly idea. Don't close your eyes or else you won't be able to read the book.

Leave your eyes completely wide open and

try to imagine what Charlie looks like.

Maybe you imagined he has blue eyes and blond hair.

Wrong!

Maybe you imagined he was tall and strong with cool sticky-up hair.

Wrong!

Maybe you imagined he has purple hair and a big furry moustache.

VERY wrong.

You're ALL wrong (apart from Evie Fairweather of 27 Wildebeest Street, Bumshufflington-on-Tweed. Well done, Evie!).

The truth is he's ALL of these descriptions. Charlie looks however you *want* him to look. He might look like the face waving back at you out of the mirror. He might look like your brother. It doesn't really matter what I say he looks like. It's what he looks like in your mind that matters.

So you go ahead and keep imagining Charlie however you want.

I realize this will make dressing up as Charlie for fancy dress very difficult. So I'll tell you one thing that *is* real about him.

He has a scar on his forehead in the shape of a lightning bolt.

What do you mean that's been done before?

It's not easy thinking of books, you know. You try writing one.

Anyway, back to Chapter 3.

CHAPTER 3 (CONTINUED)

'So . . . you're like Spider-Man?' Flora said, frowning seriously. They were all sitting in the playground in a huddle near the wooden climbing frame.

'No!' answered Charlie, slapping his forehead. 'We've been through this already. I was nothing like Spider-Man. I was a spider. I turned into a spider.'

'Hmm,' replied Flora, deep in thought. 'And you're sure you weren't dreaming?'

'Of course I'm sure!' Charlie said, clearly exasperated. 'I was nearly eaten by Chairman Meow!'

'And this happened after you got back from

hospital? From visiting your brother?'

'Yes! Straight after.'

'Hmm.' Flora rubbed her chin, thinking hard. 'Hmm.'

'What does "hmm" mean?'

'It's a noise people make when they're thinking,' Flora said in a do-you-really-not-know-that voice. 'Have you never heard someone say –'

'Yes, I know what "hmm" *actually means*. I meant, what did you mean when you hmmed. You hmmed twice.'

'Oh! I see. Well,' Flora replied, a knowing look on her face, 'I think I know what caused this.'

'You do?' Mohsen said, wide-eyed. Mohsen was often wide-eyed.

'You do?' said Wogan, normal-eyed.

'You do?' asked Charlie, narrow-eyed.

Basically there was a lot of eye action going on.

'I do. It's obvious.'

'OK then, Miss Smarty-pants, what's going on?' Mohsen said, crossing his arms.

'So, Charlie, you changed into a spider straight after you were at the hospital, correct?'

Charlie nodded. 'Yup.'

'Well . . . I think maybe when you went to

see your brother you sat on a needle and accidentally injected your bum with some sort of crazy medicine.'

'I sat on a –? I think I would have noticed if I sat on a needle and injected my bum with crazy medicine!'

'Not necessarily,' Mohsen said gravely. 'I once had an injection on my bum and I hardly felt it.'

'Exactly!' Flora thumped her palm.

'That's completely crazy!' Charlie shouted in disbelief.

'No more crazy than turning into a spider,' Flora said quickly.

Wogan and Mohsen nodded solemnly in agreement.

'OK, tell me one thing.' Charlie held up a finger to illustrate his point. 'Just tell me one thing . . . WHY WOULD A HOSPITAL HAVE CRAZY MEDICINE THAT TURNS PEOPLE

INTO SPIDERS?'

This question was met with silence.

'He has a point,' said Mohsen.

'Maybe . . .' said Wogan. 'Maybe it was medicine that was supposed to turn spiders into people and – actually, forget that.'

'Well, I don't know!' Flora held her hands

up. 'It was just a suggestion. I think the only thing we can do is keep an eye on you as much as possible, so we can pick you up and keep you safe if it happens again. And we definitely do not want this happening at the school play.'

In a few weeks Charlie was due to take a starring role in the school play as Sad Potato Number 1.

Yes, that's right. Sad Potato Number 1.

Charlie groaned. 'Oh no! I hadn't even thought of that. What happens if I change into a spider in front of the whole school?'

'Don't worry.' Flora patted Charlie's hand reassuringly. 'It probably won't happen again.'

'Yeah. I'm absolutely sure it won't happen again. But we should definitely keep an eye on you,' said Mohsen sensibly. 'You know – just in case. Except we can't do that when you're at home. So you'll have to tell your parents.'

'I can't tell my parents,' cried Charlie. 'I

tried telling my mum but she didn't believe me. And, thinking about it, I don't *want* to tell them. They've got enough to worry about. SmoothMove's got his big scan coming up soon and they're pretty worried, I think. If it doesn't go well, he'll have to have *another* operation and then he could be in hospital for ages more.'

Nobody replied for a moment.

'Look,' said Flora. 'If you want to talk about it, we're all here for you.'

Mohsen and Wogan nodded.

'No,' replied Charlie quickly, blinking. 'Thanks. I'll just have to make sure that I shut my bedroom door if it happens again. So Chairman Meow or The Great Catsby[7] don't get in.'

All agreed that this was a very sensible course of action.

---

[7] The Great Catsby was Charlie's other cat. But he was incredibly lazy and did nothing except eat and sit in a cardboard box on top of the small fridge in the kitchen. The Great Catsby was highly unlikely to leave his box, never mind run upstairs to eat a spider.

But, in fact, Charlie needn't have worried about turning into a spider at home again. What he *should* have been worrying about was turning into a pigeon at school.

Because that's exactly what happened a few days later.

CHAPTER 4

All had been quiet for a week or so. Charlie hadn't changed into any animals. School was still school. His parents were still parenting. SmoothMove was *still* in hospital waiting for his scan. Wogan and Mohsen were still slightly scared of Flora.

But on a slow Wednesday afternoon, during a times table test, it happened again.

'Hey, Charlie!'

This was Dylan. Dylan van der Gruyne was the class bully, and he hated Charlie more than anybody else in the school.

'Hey, Charlie!' Dylan whispered again loudly

'What?' Charlie whispered back, knowing

what was coming because he was talking to Dylan and Dylan never said anything nice to anybody.

'You smell like a frog's bum!'

Dylan sniggered to himself.

'No, I don't. Anyway, what does a frog's bum smell like? It might smell nice for all you know.'

Even as Charlie was saying that he realized it probably wasn't the smartest comeback.

'Hey, Teddy!' Dylan hissed at the boy next to him. Teddy was Dylan's best friend and he had a large house, and his mum drove a big Range Rover but Teddy wasn't ever allowed to call her Mum – Teddy had to call her by her

name, Lou-Lou. 'Charlie thinks frog bums smell nice. Charlie sniffs frog bums!'

Teddy burst out laughing.

'WHATISTHEMEANINGOFTHIS YOUAREDOINGATESTANDIASKED FORSILENCE.'

That was the teacher, Mr Wind. Arthur Wind was really old – forty-something – and he had grey hair and was pretty nice most of the time, apart from:

a) Whenever his football team, Birmingham United, lost.

b) Whenever Ms Fyre, the head teacher, was off sick.

c) Whenever people laughed during a test while he was on his phone sending text messages (possibly text messages to Ms Fyre, but we can't be certain about that).

They were doing a test and Mr Wind was on his phone.

'YOUKNOWIASKEDFORSILENCE
BUTICANHEARGIGGLINGWHATON
EARTHISGOINGON?'

Whenever Mr Wind was angry he spoke very fast and without punctuation. What he actually said was:

'You know I asked for silence, but I can hear giggling. What on earth is going on?'

None of the children said anything in reply.

'The next peep I hear out of anyone will have them sent quick-sharp to Ms Fyre to explain themselves.'

Ms Fyre was tall, well-dressed and huge-haired. When she smiled, which she only ever did just before she was about to explode with fury, her curled lips revealed vast pale gums and intimidating slabs of teeth. They were teeth designed for pulling chunks of meat off thigh bones. Her office was always warm and stuffy, which made sweat prickle down children's backs

53

as they stood anxiously waiting for her to speak. The oppressive heat was also perfect for the many orchid plants that were dotted around her office. The orchids were Ms Fyre's babies, and she seemed to care an awful lot more for them than she did for the children in her school. The heat and the orchids gave the office something of a jungle feel: steamy, unpleasant and somewhere you'd be lucky to get out of alive.

A moment later, something hit Charlie on the back of the head. Whatever it was, another one came, pranged off his ear and landed on the floor. It was a paper missile.

Another one hit his neck.

Dylan was pinging paper missiles at him using a rubber band as a catapult.

Charlie swung round.

'Cut it out, Dylan!' he whispered.

Dylan grinned at him. A grin that said: 'I'm really not going to cut it out, but thanks for the feedback.'

Charlie turned back to his test again.

A few seconds later, another missile hit.

'Just cut it out!' Charlie whispered, but just that little bit too loudly.

'RIGHTWHOWASTHAT,' shouted Mr Wind.

Quick as a flash came the reply from Dylan: 'It was Charlie, sir. He's trying to distract me.'

'RIGHT, CHARLIE MCGUFFIN, I WARNED YOU. YOU KNOW THE WAY TO MS FYRE'S OFFICE.'

Charlie tried protesting. 'But, sir –'

'Now, McGuffin!' Mr Wind pointed to the door.

Charlie really tried, but he couldn't help the prickling in his eyes turning to tears as he walked to the door. He risked a glance at Flora, who gave him a sympathetic smile, and that was it – the tears started flowing. As he shut the door behind him he could feel Dylan's smug smile burning into him.

Charlie's head hung low as he trudged down the corridor. Being sent to Ms Fyre meant a letter home to his parents.

OUT.

They had enough to worry about with his brother, and now he was in deep trouble at school. He could already see the disappointment in their eyes. The thought made his stomach squirm and his heart begin to pound.

And that's when his left eye started twitching.

Charlie didn't think anything of it until the twitch spread to his other eye. Then, with a surge of horror, he realized what was coming. He was changing again.

The feeling burst through his whole body like an electric flower. It exploded inside him. Every part of his body was aflame, but with a fire that was squeezed and crushed through his veins and arteries and back out through every pore of his skin.

With considerable alarm Charlie saw he was growing feathers. *Feathers!* And the floor was coming towards him fast, which meant he was getting smaller. His legs were growing skinny, and attached to the bottom of the skinny legs were red feet.

And with a flap he saw that he had wings. He had *wings*.

A scream suddenly pierced his ears.

Ms Fyre was striding towards him, a look of total disgust on her face.

Charlie flapped in panic, and Ms Fyre gave another squeal of disgust. She had her arms spread, trying to corner him.

A door suddenly opened next to him. It was Maisie Wand from 1F and as soon as she saw Bird-Charlie she ran off down the corridor screaming. The door was swinging closed, but Charlie saw his opportunity and flapped his way through.

It was a bathroom. With another flap Charlie hopped on to the edge of the sink. And there, reflecting back at Charlie from the mirror, was a bird – a plump grey bird with an iridescent purple-and-green neck.

Charlie was a *pigeon*.

The door burst open and Ms Fyre stalked in, edging round Charlie to open the window. Then she started waving her arms at Charlie, trying to force him out.

Charlie didn't need any more encouragement. With one beat of his wings he was at the window, and with another he was out and into the playground.

He was free! He had escaped!

He was a *pigeon*!

Settling on the tarmac, Charlie bobbed uncertainly forward, unsure of what to do with himself. Before he had time to gather his thoughts a startling flap of wings nearly made him jump out of his feathers.

Another pigeon had landed next to him. It was pacing back and forth around him, head bobbing, neck feathers glinting in the sunshine. It had gnarled toes and one foot was just a stump, like a lump of popcorn. Its eyes, little black holes in burnt orange, were – and Charlie could not mistake this – staring straight at him. The pigeon cooed, deep and low, and to Charlie's utter shock he realized it was *talking* to him. He could *understand* pigeon. And the first words that he heard the other pigeon say were:

''Allo, you beautiful, delightful little pigeon. My name is Jean-Claude. I am a pigeon. And I am in love with you.'

Charlie wasn't sure he heard him right.

'I . . . I beg your pardon?' Charlie replied. He actually cooed, which came as something of a surprise to Charlie.

'I said, my name is Jean-Claude the pigeon. And I am in love with you. You are the most beautiful pigeon I have ever seen. In the last minute.'

Charlie was beginning to wish that he did not understand pigeons.

'But-but . . .' Charlie stammered, edging away from Jean-Claude.

'Do not "but" me, *mon petit pigeon*,' Jean-Claude cooed, edging closer. 'Ours is a love that pigeons will talk of for many years. It is a story as old as time – ooh, look! What is this I spy?' Jean-Claude eyed the ground beadily. 'It is a delicious and tasty morsel of food!'

Jean-Claude pecked at some-thing, and chewed it for a few moments.

It was a small piece of gravel. 'Ah! Perhaps not so delicious, after all. Not as delicious as you, my beautiful, delectable pigeon. Now fly away with me!'

'But we've only just met!' Charlie cooed in alarm.

'Ah, but what is time? Time is an illusion! It is capricious like the – ooh, look!' Jean-Claude eyed the ground again. 'A delicious and tasty morsel of food!'

Jean-Claude pecked at something.

It was an old piece of chewing gum that stuck to his beak.

'Mmph! Mmhaphs mmoh mpho mmaphy mmapheh mmah!'

A small battle ensued as Jean-Claude attempted to dislodge the gum. Finally he succeeded.

'I said "Ah!

Perhaps not so tasty, after all!"' He flapped his foot frantically at the gum that was now stuck to the end of a claw. 'No matter! We have wasted enough time. We must make haste –'

Another flap of wings startled Charlie and Jean-Claude.

It was a second pigeon. This one was grimy-looking, with greasy feathers. And he was looking right at Charlie, with a beady look in his eye and a greedy look on his beak.

'*Bonjour!* My name is Antoine! I am a pigeon. And I am in love with you, my feathery little pigeon.'

'Oh, for goodness' sake!' Charlie exclaimed.

'I am also looking out for any small pieces of food. I am particularly looking for crumbs,' Antoine the pigeon said.

'Back off, Monsieur Antoine! This pigeon is mine!' Jean-Claude flapped angrily. 'We have been in love for minutes! And any crumbs in this particular region are mine too.'

Antoine bustled. '*Monsieur*, you are not the emperor of crumbs! And you are not the emperor of this exquisite pigeon's heart, for it is I, Antoine the pigeon, pecker of crumbs and –'

At that, a sudden flap of wings announced the arrival of – you guessed it – ANOTHER pigeon.

'Did somebody mention crumbs? I am – *zut alors!*' The new pigeon bobbed towards Charlie. 'But who are you? What a fine example of pigeon you are! We must fly away together, you and I! A love like ours cannot wait! But first we must eat crumbs!'

'Stay away, new pigeon! This beautiful pigeon and all crumbs in this general area are mine!' Jean-Claude flapped excitedly.

''ow dare you?' Antoine cooed, puffing out his chest. 'This is MY pigeon. But I am prepared to discuss sharing the crumbs in this general area.'

As a heated argument began to break out, Charlie took the opportunity to escape. He walked away, head bobbing, edging as slyly as possible away from the bickering pigeons. He had made it a few metres without getting noticed. And then all the pigeons turned as one.

'*Ma chérie!*'

'Do not go! I am just a foolish love-struck pigeon!'

'We must fly away together, you and I, to pigeon paradise!'

The three pigeons strutted menacingly towards Charlie.

Charlie bobbed backwards away from them.

They strutted quicker, circling him now.

Charlie panicked, as Charlie usually did these days, and he flapped his wings.

He lifted into the air. He flapped more, and rose higher, but the other pigeons took flight too.

'Come back! We fly together!' they called in unison.

Charlie beat his wings harder, rising above the school now. The others followed, though, flying round Charlie, trying to force him down. Charlie pushed his way through the circling pigeons, climbing higher still.

'Some crumbs!' cried Antoine suddenly. 'I'm certain I see some crumbs of food in the general area below!'

'We must peck at the delicious crumbs!' chorused the other pigeons in reply.

And with that all three pigeons flew to the ground and began pecking, leaving Charlie flying alone.

He was flying.

Charlie was *flying*.

With a rush of joy and surprise he realized he was soaring way above the school now. He beat his wings harder, the wind whistling through his feathers. Higher and higher Charlie flew, so free, his heart bursting with happiness.

Silence. The rush of traffic was gone, and there was just the sound of the gentle breeze lifting him.

Charlie had never felt so exhilarated in his life.

Below him he felt, rather than saw, a map, a magnetic map, a rippling field gently pulling him one way, then another.

Higher he flew, towards thick white clouds.

The air smelled icy and crisp.

Far below him, the town looked tiny. Fields stretched away towards the horizon. The earth curved gently in the distance.

Charlie hung there, softly beating his wings, suspended by the flowing currents in the air, a mile above the ground.

It was therefore perhaps the worst possible time to feel a charge of electricity shoot through him. A charge of electricity that could only mean one thing.

Charlie was changing.

Back into a boy.

A mile above the ground.

This time, Charlie had no time to panic. He knew he had to do something and do it very, very, very quickly.

He folded his wings, pointed his beak towards the ground and started diving, as fast as he could.

Down he plummeted, his eyes streaming.

500 metres to go . . .

He could feel his face changing. His feet changing.

There was the school, screaming towards him.

300 metres . . .

He felt his feathers disappearing.

Close to the ground. Hurtling down. He had to slow himself. Or the crash would be the last thing he ever did.

200 metres to go . . .

He opened his wings, tried slowing himself, and pulled out of the dive.

100 metres . . .

A lurch upwards.

50 metres . . .

He could feel his wings vanishing.

25 metres . . .

Had to land. Had to –

Charlie crashed on to the ground and rolled. And then just lay there, looking up at the sky he had just been flying in. He wasn't quite sure if he was still alive. He seemed to be – he could see the clouds rolling across the sky, and his bum hurt where he'd landed on it, but he was breathing.

He tried sitting up. He was just about OK. He looked around. By some miracle he had landed in the school field, not far from the bike and scooter rack.

'Charles McGuffin, what do you think you are doing out there?!'

A shout came from an open door. And the shout came from Ms Fyre, hands on hips, her wild bonnet of hair getting wilder by the second.

'Come on, boy, get up! What on earth are you doing just sitting there on the ground? Where have you been? Mr Wind sent you to my office AGES ago! You are in very SERIOUS trouble, young man! COME WITH ME NOW.'

Half an hour later, Charlie was walking back into his class, Ms Fyre's furious telling-off ringing in his ears, and a punishment letter in his pocket, which his parents had to sign. The thought of taking home the news of how much trouble he was in – even more since the pigeon incident – was making him feel sick. His mum and dad had enough problems without him adding to them. He'd let them down. He couldn't help it – he could feel the tears coming again. It didn't help that Dylan was staring at him with a look on his face that was a mixture of gloating and disbelief.

Wogan, Mohsen and Flora were looking at him too, clearly wondering what had happened. He'd tell them later. Charlie slumped to his desk, staring at the whiteboard, trying to hide his face as tears begin to trickle down his cheeks for the second time that day.

CHAPTER 5

'**n**o way! It happened again?' Wogan said, chasing after Charlie as Charlie stormed off ahead of him across the playground.

'Yes,' said Charlie glumly.

'While you were on your way to Ms Fyre? You turned into a pigeon?'

'Yes!' said Charlie, frustration creeping into his voice.

'Hmm,' said Flora.

'Oh, don't you start hmming again. I had enough of that last time.'

'Well, one way or another, we need to get to the bottom of it.'

'No, what we really need to do is work out

how to stop my parents from murdering me when they see this punishment letter.' Charlie pulled the letter out of his pocket. 'Listen to what it says: "Disobedience, lying, evasiveness and all manner of general misdemeanours." What am I supposed to do about all that? I'm dead.'

'Good question,' said Wogan, sounding full of action. 'OK, firstly, who is Miss Demeanours? Is she a new teacher? And *General* Miss Demeanours? Why is the army involved? We need to know.'

Mohsen looked at Charlie and rolled his eyes. Charlie smiled for the first time in quite a while.

The four were quiet for a moment, each lost in thought, until Flora broke the silence.

'It's funny that it happened . . .' Flora paused carefully. 'You know, when you were by yourself. Again,' she added. 'It's just, you know, a bit strange.'

Charlie narrowed his eyes. 'What do you mean "funny"? Strange how?'

Mohsen and Wogan held their breath.

'It's just that, well, nobody else has actually *seen* it happen yet,' Flora said slowly and gently.

'I knew it!' Charlie shouted. 'You don't believe me! You think I'm lying!'

'I don't think you're lying!' Flora protested.

'You do! I can't believe, after everything that's happened, one of my best friends thinks I'm making it all up.'

'I don't!'

'Then what *do* you think?'

'Well, have you considered that perhaps you just *think* it's happening? Maybe your brain is tricking you? The mind is a funny thing and I know you *believe* you changed into a spider and a pigeon but maybe it didn't . . . actually . . . happen?'

Silence hit the four of them again.

Charlie looked furious.

Flora looked like she'd just broken the news to her pet hamster, Rollo, who was two years old, that hamsters usually only live for two years.

Mohsen and Wogan looked terrified.

'Well, you two are being very quiet. What do you think? Do you believe me?' Charlie glared at Mohsen and Wogan.

Mohsen and Wogan sort of muttered and shrugged. They looked nervously at the ground.

Charlie rounded on them, his face red.

'Well, that's just great. Fantastic. Not one of my so-called best friends believes me. Well, you can all just be friends without me.'

And with that Charlie stormed off to the other side of the playground.

He sat on an empty bench fuming silently. And as he sat there, watching a football game between some Year Twos, his anger slowly turned into something much, much worse.

Loneliness.

His stomach felt hollow and yet at the same time like it was full of squirming worms. His head was throbbing and his face was hot and his

eyes were prickling with tears again. He wanted to get a hug from his mum or play *Pokémon* with Mohsen or football with Flora or wrestle with Wogan or see SmoothMove again or anything, anything to make this awful feeling disappear.

There really is nothing lonelier, Charlie thought glumly to himself, *than sitting by yourself in a packed playground.* He closed his eyes, if only to stop himself from crying for the third time that day.

'I saw you.'

Charlie swung round at the voice, startled.

It was Dylan.

'What do *you* want?' Charlie said, having thought his day couldn't get any worse.

'I saw you,' Dylan said again.

'What do you mean you saw me?' Charlie said, eyes slanting with suspicion.

'You know what I mean,' Dylan replied.

'Er, no, I don't, actually,' Charlie said, getting more frustrated.

'Yes, you *do*.'

'Look. If I did, I wouldn't ask you, would I?'

'If you call me wood-eye again, I'll thump you.'

'What?! I didn't call you wood-eye! I meant "would I?"!'

'You're just saying the same thing. Anyway, the point is: I. Saw. You.'

'SAW ME WHAT?' shouted Charlie.

'Fall from the sky,' said Dylan.

'Oh! You saw *that*!' cried Charlie, relief flooding him. Not only did he finally understand what Dylan was going on about, but he also had proof that he wasn't going insane.

'What else did you think I'd be talking about? Have you done anything else worth talking about?'

'I guess not.'

'Exactly. Well, I was staring out of the window after you got sent to Ms Fyre and I just saw this thing falling out of the sky. It had wings but then it didn't, and it was too big for a bird, and then it hit the floor and sat up and that was when I saw. Saw it was you. I mean, I always knew you were a freak, but not this much of a freak.'

'I can't believe it! Finally someone has seen me change! I felt like I was going crazy.'

'Calm down, freak boy. So can you just change into whatever you want?'

'I wish,' said Charlie. 'I just sort of change into animals at random. I can't control it. It's useless really. Not exactly a superhero, am I?'

'Hmm. Maybe not.' Dylan thought for a moment. 'Did you poo on anybody's head when you were up there?'

'No. I was waiting for you to come out of class but I changed back before I had the chance,' Charlie said, grinning.

Charlie saw a reluctant smile creep on to Dylan's face.

'And now none of my friends believe me.'

Dylan snorted. 'I don't blame them. If I hadn't seen it, I'd think you'd lost the plot.'

'I guess so . . . But it doesn't matter now. You can tell them what you saw.'

'I'm afraid not.' Dylan shook his head with a hint of sadness.

'But . . . but why not?'

'I'm sorry.' Dylan turned as if to walk away. 'I can't.'

'But why not?'

'Because, Charlie, you're missing the obvious. We hate each other.'

'I don't hate you! I mean, we're never going to be best of friends, but . . . hate?' Charlie was starting to get a sinking feeling that Dylan was perhaps the worst person who could have seen him change.

'Oh, come on. Face the truth. You and I are mortal enemies. We always have been. We always will be. And now YOU have some sort of freakish ability. And that means that I have to try to destroy you.'

'Why are you sounding like a villain in a movie?'

'Maybe I have to build a robot suit or swallow some radiation to defeat you,' Dylan said to himself. 'I'll have to start saving for a lair.'

'OK, that's really not helping the whole movie-villain thing. We don't have to be enemies, you know.'

'Oh, but we do,' replied Dylan. 'We *are* enemies, Charlie, and we can never forget that. We are destined to fight. That's just how stories work, and there's nothing either of us can do about it.'

'But we don't *have* to be! We can be *friends*.'

'Come now. Where's the fun in that?' Dylan gave a wolfish grin and then walked off towards the classrooms.

Charlie watched Dylan disappear into the distance and shook his head.

'What a total nutcase.'

★★★

It wasn't until the next day that Charlie spoke to Mohsen, Wogan and Flora again. He had spent a miserable evening at home, banished to his room and banned from his PlayStation after delivering his punishment letter to his mum and dad. They had been very, very angry.

'I'm disappointed in you, Charlie McGuffin,' Charlie's dad had said. He'd actually looked disappointed too. Usually his father was good-humoured; even when he was telling him off, Charlie could always see a gleam in his dad's eyes. But since SmoothMove had gone into hospital, the gleam wasn't there so much.

'We both are. *Very* disappointed,' said Charlie's mum. 'But we both still love you very much,' she added, giving Charlie a warm smile and a lump in his throat.

Charlie had sat in his room for the rest of the evening, simmering with misery, anger, loneliness and, worse than all of those – guilt.

His brother was due to have his big scan in two weeks' time and Charlie felt desperate for making his parents angry.

So, when Mohsen, Wogan and Flora all came up to him in the playground first thing the next day, his heart pounded with joy. But he couldn't show that.

'Hey,' said Flora.

'Hey,' said Charlie quietly.

'Hey,' said Mohsen and Wogan.

'Hey,' said Charlie back.

'So . . .' said Flora. 'We've been talking and

we thought that maybe we should say sorry.'

'Yeah?' said Charlie hopefully. He didn't really care about the apology; he just needed his friends back.

'We should have believed what you said. We should have trusted you. And we're sorry. Sorry.'

'Yeah,' said Mohsen. 'Sorry.'

'Soz,' said Wogan.

Charlie's heart swelled. He felt it might burst out of his chest with happiness.

'You know what? I don't blame you guys. It IS mad. I wouldn't believe me either. I'd think I was bananas too, if I was you. So let's just forget about it, OK? And hey – guess what?'

'What?' they all replied excitedly.

'You won't believe who can actually prove my story is real . . .'

CHAPTER 6

'I can't believe who can actually prove your story is real,' said Flora, with a disbelieving shake of the head.

'Nor can I,' said Mohsen, also with a disbelieving shake of the head.

'I actually *can*. I believe you, Charlie,' said Wogan, scowling at Mohsen and Flora. 'I mean, come on, guys – it's terrible that, after all that apologizing, you're saying you don't believe Charlie again. We've been through this.'

'No! We do believe Charlie! It was just a phrase. We only meant it's surprising that it's Dylan,' said Flora.

Wogan looked slightly blanker than usual, if possible.

'Never mind, Wogan,' Flora said, looking at him like he was a puppy with three legs learning to walk. 'Anyway,' she continued, 'we now know that Charlie changing wasn't just a one-off. It's happened twice. Charlie – you need help. We need to work out what exactly is going on with you. And then maybe we can find a cure. So I have constructed a plan. We are going to use Science!'

'Yes!' said Mohsen, thumping a fist into his palm.

'Yes!' said Charlie, clapping his hands.

'Yes!' said Wogan. 'Of course! We can draw a picture of the water cycle! And then we can – hang on, what use is science?'

'Because, Wogan, science is what we use when there is a mystery,' replied Flora patiently. 'Science gives us answers to questions. If it

wasn't for science we'd still be living in caves, spending all day hunting sabre-tooth tigers and lying around in mammoth-wool underpants.'

'That actually sounds pretty wicked-cool,' replied Wogan.

The others couldn't help but agree.

'*And* there'd be no school,' Wogan continued. 'And we wouldn't have to get jobs when we're older. In fact, I don't think I like science very much.'

Flora sighed.

'What about medicine? And space travel? And the internet? Or PlayStation? That's ALL science. And now we're going to use science to work out what on earth is happening to Charlie,' Flora said firmly.

'And we need to do it super-fast too,' agreed Mohsen. 'You know, before Charlie changes again. In case he doesn't change back to a human.'

Charlie groaned. 'Oh, thanks a bunch, Mohsen. I hadn't even thought of *that* happening. That's ANOTHER thing for me to worry about. But you're right. We need to work out what's going on quickly. It's the school play in two weeks, and I can't be turning into an animal in front of the whole school.'

'The school play where you're starring as Sad Potato Number 1?' said Mohsen.

'Yes. That's right, Mohsen. The school play where I'm starring as Sad Potato Number 1,' replied Charlie. 'It's an important role. Do you have anything to say about that?'

'No,' Mohsen replied in a small voice.

'Well, it might be good if you *did* change,' Wogan said. 'You know, if you became a tiger or a *T. rex* or something and scared everyone away, then at least I wouldn't have to do my final song and kiss Cara Cotton.'

'Don't be daft, Wogan,' said Flora. 'We've been through this before. It would *not* be good *at all*. What will happen to Charlie if he suddenly turns into an animal in front of the whole school?'

'He could do a poo on –'

'No, Wogan. You are poo-*obsessed*. I'll tell you what will happen. If Charlie changes into an animal at the play, the teachers will call the police and the police will call the government and the government will call the scientists. And then Charlie will get taken away and experimented on. He'll get *operated* on, Wogan. *Dissected*.'

'THANK YOU VERY MUCH BUT CAN YOU ALL STOP GIVING ME NEW THINGS TO WORRY ABOUT THAT I HADN'T EVEN THOUGHT OF!'
Charlie shouted.

'Don't panic,' said Flora confidently. 'We're going to use science so you don't have to worry!'

'So . . .' Wogan was thinking hard. 'We're going to use science to stop the scientists? If science is so good, shouldn't we just, you know . . .?'

'No, I don't know, Wogan,' said Flora, getting more and more agitated. 'Are you suggesting we hand Charlie over to scientists? So they can cut him into tiny pieces and examine him under a microscope?'

'CAN YOU ALL STOP TALKING IMMEDIATELY NOW PLEASE!' Charlie yelled.

'Right,' said Flora, ignoring Charlie. 'So here's my plan. We need to find out WHAT causes the change in Charlie. We know it isn't light because it has happened during the day and the night. We know it isn't heat because it wasn't really hot or cold when it happened last time. I have also ruled out electricity, radiation and space dust.'

'How have you ruled out space dust?' asked Mohsen, looking puzzled.

'Don't ask questions. It's just science, OK?' said Flora dismissively. 'We can discount animal bites, because you turned into a bird. Unless you have been bitten by a bird recently and forgotten to mention it?'

'I haven't,' Charlie said.

'You haven't been shot with a laser or struck by lightning?'

'Uh, no,' Charlie said, shaking his head.

'You haven't been given a magic ring?'

'Nope.'

'Or been part of an experimental army programme?'

'What? No!'

'And you definitely haven't been kidnapped by space aliens?'

'Do you not think I might have mentioned that before?' replied Charlie. 'Do you not think I might have said, "Oh, hey, guys, guess what, I got kidnapped by space aliens last night"? No! I have not been kidnapped by space aliens!'

'That you know of,' said Wogan with a
meaningful look.

'What?' said Charlie.

'You might have been asleep. Or the aliens
might have wiped your memory. That's what
happened to my Uncle Harry in America. Wiped
his memory completely.'

'Then how did he remember that aliens kidnapped him?' asked Mohsen.

'Because he was found in the neighbours' barn wearing just his wellies and he couldn't remember how he got there. So it must have been aliens.'

'We are getting distracted,' said Flora.

'We are going to have to assume that it wasn't aliens, because we have no *evidence* that they kidnapped Charlie.'

'OK. Well, that's a lot of things that it isn't. What do you think it *is*?' asked Charlie.

'Well – and there's no easy way to say this, Charlie – I think you're a mutant. A genetic freak of nature.'

'Thanks a bunch, Flora.'

'No. It's cool. The closest comparison I can make is the Incredible Hulk. When he is angry he turns into a big green monster. I think what's happening with you is that when you're scared you turn into an animal.'

Mohsen, Wogan and Charlie stood in silence for a moment, taking this in.

'You see,' continued Flora, 'you were scared of having to see Ms Fyre and you were even more scared about having to tell your parents, so you turned into a pigeon. And you first changed into a spider after you visited your brother in hospital and found out about his scan and the operation and obviously . . .' Flora let the sentence hang in the air unfinished.

Charlie squirmed uncomfortably. 'Hmm. OK, let's say it's true. I'm not saying it is, but let's just say it is. How do we test your theory?' he asked.

'Ah!' said Flora, one finger pointing in the air. 'That's the fun bit.'

CHAPTER 7

It was a beautiful Saturday morning. The sun was shining, just the odd small white cloud scudding high across the sky. It was not the sort of day that Charlie felt like facing pretty certain death.

But we don't always get what we want in life.

And Charlie was finding that out the hard way.

'This really, really, REALLY does not feel safe at all, guys.'

The four were at the top of Bandit's Hill. Bandit's Hill was the hill in their local park. It was high and steep, and commanded beautiful views of the surrounding countryside.

But Charlie didn't really care that the hill commanded beautiful views of the surrounding countryside right now, thank you very much, because right now Charlie was at the very top of the hill, sitting in a dilapidated old go-kart.

Wogan's dad had made the go-kart a few years ago, and Wogan's dad was not a good go-kart maker.

In fact, it would be fair to say that Wogan's dad was the worst go-kart maker ever to actually make a go-kart.[8] He had essentially attached a pair of wheels to each end of a box. There wasn't even a steering wheel. There, however, a brake, which was just a stick that, when pushed, merely dragged along the ground. Or, more accurately, there had been a brake, but Flora had spent the last twenty minutes carefully unscrewing it. When the go-kart was finally brake-less, Flora announced that the experiment was ready.

Staring down at the very steep, very long and very bumpy descent in front of him gave Charlie a weird feeling in his stomach and his bum. Ahead of him he saw, at best, severe injury, and, at worst, a tragic end to his brief life. And one child in hospital was enough for his parents, Charlie thought.

---

[8] Wogan's dad was also the worst namer of children. He had meant to call Wogan *Logan*, after Wolverine's real name, but after one too many whiskies he had got confused and accidentally named him after an old BBC presenter instead.

'You want me to go down the hill in this . . .
this box-on-wheels WITHOUT any brakes?
That is deadly dangerous, Flora.'

'Don't be daft, Charlie!' said Flora. 'It is *not*
deadly dangerous!'

It was deadly dangerous.

'But this thing,' said Charlie, pointing around
him at the go-kart, 'is an absolute deathtrap.'

'Oh, Charlie!' said Flora. 'It is *not* an absolute
deathtrap!'

It was an absolute deathtrap.

'Look,' continued Flora. 'It's the only way
to find out for certain whether my theory is
correct. We need you to be scared. If it had
brakes, you wouldn't be scared.'

'But I don't want to die,' said Charlie in a
small voice.

'Pull yourself together, Charlie,' said
Flora, sounding increasingly exasperated. 'Do
you really think I would put you in any real

danger just to prove a theory?'

'I guess not . . .'

She absolutely would.

'Exactly. Do you think Neil Armstrong and Buzz Aldrin were scared when they went to the moon? Probably, but they did it anyway, because it was for the good of mankind. And if we can prove my theory and actually *observe* you change into an animal, it will be like landing on the moon, Charlie.'

Mohsen and Wogan just stood there in noticeable silence. Their faces, though, betrayed a mixture of guilt, fear and panic.

'OK . . . OK. Let's do it,' said Charlie, deeply uncertain. It was impossible to say no to Flora.

'Awesome! You're super-brave, Charlie! I knew you'd do it! You're a hero.'

Against his better judgement, Charlie felt a glow in his chest and started blushing at Flora's words.

'Pass me the helmet!' said Charlie.

'Passing you the helmet, sir!' said Flora.

Charlie tied the helmet on, and gripped the side of the deathtrap go-kart. He let go for a short moment to give a proud salute to his friends. Mohsen and Wogan gave solemn, mournful salutes back. Flora bent behind the go-kart and gripped it, ready to start pushing.

Charlie swallowed, a ball of terror rolling in his stomach.

There was a moment of perfect silence.

The world held its breath.

Just the wind softly ruffling Charlie's hair.

Parp!

That was Charlie, accidentally letting out a little terror-fart.

Flora, who was bent down directly behind Charlie's bum, grimaced.

'Ugh, Charlie!'

But then, with as much strength as he

could muster, Charlie shouted through his fear.

'Go!'

At Charlie's word, Flora began running as fast as she could, pushing the go-kart and Charlie down the hill. Almost immediately Charlie was going so fast that Flora couldn't keep up and had to let go. She stood, watching proudly as Charlie disappeared at a quite alarming speed.

Meanwhile, as Charlie started speeding down the hill, a number of thoughts came very, very quickly to his mind. They were:

1. He was travelling very, very fast – much faster than he thought was possible in a go-kart – and he was absolutely going to die.

2. He should not have had the vanilla milkshake and apple juice before he attempted the ride. It was now sloshing about in his stomach

and he was almost certainly going to puke before he died. If he ever did this again, which he would NEVER, EVER do, he would learn from this mistake.

3. He should have brought a cushion because every single jolt and judder of the deathtrap go-kart was causing his bum to bang on the wooden base of the barf-inducing, bum-banging, kamikaze death-machine go-kart, and he was now going to die with a really sore bum. Covered in barf.

Charlie was now pretty experienced in what to do in emergency situations such as this, where he was in grave personal danger.

And that was to panic.

'F L A R G G L E - W A R R R B L L E - F N A R G G H G H - G U - G U - G U - G U - G U - WAARRGH!' he screamed.

'GUUUUUUUUUUUURGHHH-GUH-

GUH-GUH-BABABABABAB-
FWURNGHHHHHHH!' he continued.

Now obviously this wasn't what Charlie
intended to shout. But the combination of the
shaking and shuddering kart, the wind blowing
into his wide-open mouth, and the terror of
barfing and imminent death meant his words

came out sounding like a big hairy baboon doing a massive fart in the bath.

It is unfortunately not possible to provide a direct translation of what Charlie was trying to say, because half of the words he was attempting to scream were words that would get an immediate and extremely severe punishment from his parents. And probably from your parents too. And my parents as well, actually, so I'm certainly not going to write them down here. If I did, I'd probably get in trouble with all parents everywhere, and that's the last thing anybody would want to deal with. Can you imagine being in trouble with ALL parents EVERYWHERE? Sheesh.

So, the polite, parent-friendly translation of what Charlie screamed was:

'GOODNESS GRACIOUS ME, I AM IN QUITE CONSIDERABLE FEAR FOR MY LIFE AND I SINCERELY REGRET

AGREEING TO PARTAKE IN THIS LUDICROUS SCHEME!' he screamed.

'I WOULD VERY MUCH LIKE TO EXIT THIS GO-KART NOW BEFORE I SUFFER, AT BEST, SERIOUS INJURY AND, AT WORST, DEATH. AND I FEEL I MIGHT BE ABOUT TO BE SICK. AND MY BOTTOM IS IN A GREAT DEAL OF PAIN!' he continued.

Screaming, however, was doing little to help Charlie's perilous situation. And frankly there was very little he *could* do that would help his perilous situation. Impossibly he was going faster than before. People were literally diving out of the way of the out-of-control, rampaging go-kart. Dogs were chasing Charlie, barking furiously as they raced behind him, but they were losing the race. Other people were using their phones to record the scene. The videos were immediately uploaded to YouTube with titles like *'Insane boy flying downhill in deadly* go-kart', 'Mad screaming kid faces certain death in deathtrap' and 'Boy does nervous little fart in a kart then screams gibberish'. Before he was halfway down the hill Charlie was already famous on the internet.

But by the time Charlie was halfway down the hill that's not what Charlie was thinking about. By that time Charlie was unable to think any thoughts at all. The speed at which he was now travelling made thought impossible. The

world had reduced to a blur. It was only as he approached the bottom of Bandit's Hill at roughly the speed of a space rocket that another thought sprang into his mind, and it was that he was about to get very wet.

At the bottom of the hill was a short stretch of grass, with a number of people stretched out on it, enjoying the early-morning sunshine.

And beyond that was Bandit's Lake.

It was a small lake. More of a pond, really. But it was cold. And full of ducks. And Charlie was headed straight for it.

How neither Flora, Mohsen, Wogan nor Charlie had realized that hurtling straight into the water was the most likely outcome of his ride was a mystery that should be analysed in depth, if he survived.

But now was not the time.

Charlie hit the bottom of the hill faster than a cheetah running for an ice-cream van on the hottest day of the year.

More people dived out the way, screaming, as he barrelled towards them. He crashed through a picnic, squashing sandwiches and knocking over drinks. A kite, ripped from the hands of a terrified child, got caught in the wheels of the kart, and fluttered behind it as he plunged towards the lake.

Charlie closed his eyes.

The kart hit a small rise just before the edge,

and flew into the air.

It hung there for the briefest second, like a mad, out-of-control deathtrap go-kart hanging in the air.

Ducks scattered, quacking in terror, not quite believing that a small boy in a go-kart was about to plunge into their pond.

An almighty splash.

The cold hit Charlie and took his breath away.

He bobbed to the surface, gasping for breath, and swam as quickly as he could for shore. He crawled out, reeds plastered to his head, and collapsed on to his back, panting and staring into the blue sky. Mutters of disbelief and shock rumbled through the crowd gathering around him.

He let the sun warm his skin and his soaking clothes.

It was then that the realization sank in.

He hadn't changed into an animal.

Flora was wrong.

They still had no idea why he was changing.

And he only had a week and a half until the school play.

CHAPTER 8

'**Y**ou *are* joking?!' Charlie said in utter disbelief.

'It's the ONLY explanation,' Flora said, crossing her arms.

It was Monday lunch break, and the first time the four had been together since the Bandit's Hill Disaster.

'You're saying I wasn't scared enough to change? You are actually completely and totally – DO YOU REALIZE HOW TERRIFIED I WAS?'

'I think you enjoyed yourself too much,' Flora said thoughtfully, as much to herself as anyone else.

'You have lost it. Like actually properly lost it,' Charlie replied.

'She might have a point,' said Mohsen. 'It did look awesome wicked fun.'

'I can assure you it was NOT.'

'Charlie,' said Wogan, placing a hand on Charlie's shoulder. 'You were whooping with delight. The whole way down.'

'That was NOT whooping! I was screaming!' protested Charlie.

'We could hear you, Charlie. Whooping.'

'Screaming!'

'Whooping.'

'I. WAS. SCREAMING. SCREAMING! I THOUGHT I WAS GOING TO DIE. I WAS TERRIFIED.'

'Hmm,' said Flora.

'Oh, do not start hmming!' snapped Charlie.

'We should listen to Flora's hmms. You know that,' Mohsen said.

'Hmm,' Flora hmmed again. 'I think I might have made a mistake.'

'YES, I KNOW!' said Charlie.

'I should have thought more carefully,' continued Flora.

'You're absolutely right there,' said Charlie.

'Charlie, you had rollercoaster fear.'

'Rollercoaster fear?' Charlie replied, shaking his head. But there was something that nagged in the back of his mind. Deep down – deep, deep down – Charlie knew there had been a tiny element of excitement in his descent down Bandit's Hill. Looking back, Charlie realized that as well as ludicrously dangerous and terrifying and insane, it had been . . . *fun*.

'The first time you changed, you were worried about your brother. The second time it happened, you were in trouble at school. You were upset and anxious both times. There was nothing enjoyable about that. Worry isn't fun. And that's where the experiment went wrong.'

'And so . . .?' said Charlie, nervous of the reply.

'And so we need to do another experiment to test the improved theory,' said Flora, with an air of finality. 'That's how science works, Charlie.'

'OK then, smarty-pants, what's your plan this time?'

Flora stroked her chin. 'I haven't quite finalized it yet. It's nearly there. But not quite. But I will definitely have a plan before you change again. One hundred per cent definite,' said Flora with an air of confidence and certainty.

Behind the four friends, clearly looking very pleased at what he had just overheard, Dylan crept off silently, unnoticed.

★★★

Perhaps Charlie shouldn't have been quite so willing to believe Flora's confidence and certainty. Two days after their conversation, her plan was still yet to appear, and it was the day of the dress rehearsal for the play.

Ms Fyre and Mr Wind had spent many long evenings together writing their musical masterpiece, *The Veg of Reason*, the story of two rival gangs of vegetables, and two star-crossed vegetables from those rival gangs who fall in love and –

Actually there's no need to say anything more about the plot. There's really no point in destroying your brain cells by giving you any more details. All you need to know is that Ms Fyre and Mr Wind were very proud of it and were *extremely* anxious that everything should go as smoothly as possible at the dress rehearsal.

About twenty children were waiting backstage, all dressed in vegetable costumes and chatting and

giggling excitedly. Mohsen and Flora had decided against auditioning for the play. Wogan, though, had gone along to the audition to give Charlie moral support, and had been accidentally auditioned and cast as the main star. He was dressed as a big stalk of broccoli and was sweating under the heavy costume at the thought of having to kiss Cara Cotton at the end of the play. Cara was sitting opposite him, nervously adjusting her cauliflower costume.

Charlie sat on the floor looking very glum. This look was perfect for his role as Sad Potato

Number 1, and Mr Wind seemed very happy to see Charlie getting into his character so well. Charlie sank further into the floor when he heard Cara's cue to go on.

Dylan, dressed in a bright orange costume, was also getting perfectly into his role as Happy Carrot Number 2. He sauntered up to Charlie with a huge grin stretched across his face.

'Cheer up, Charlie,' sneered Dylan. 'It's not the end of the world. It's not like you're about to change into an animal and be revealed as a freak of nature and sent to the circus. Oh, sorry! I forgot. Yes you are. That's exactly what's going to happen. Say goodbye to your life, loser.'

'Oh, get lost, Dylan. I'm really not in the mood.'

Dylan gave him a smug smile in return and sauntered off. Charlie *hated* happy carrots.

A moment later, he heard Cara Cotton singing her cauliflower song. That meant he and Dylan were up next. They both went into the wings and waited for Cara's song to end. Cara finished, bowed and that was their cue. She came past looking relieved. Charlie tried to walk on, but Dylan pushed him out of the way.

'You're going to change!' he whispered at Charlie as he shoved past.

A ball of nervousness bounced in Charlie's stomach.

'Shut up, Dylan. Just shut up.'

They walked out on to the stage. Mr Wind and Ms Fyre were sat next to each other in the front row, looking expectantly up at Charlie and Dylan. Mr Wind gave them the thumbs up, and Ms Fyre bared her tombstone teeth to remind them to smile. Quite why a sad potato was supposed to smile was lost on Charlie.

Dylan coughed, did an awkward bow, and then began to sing his 'Happy Carrot'[9] song:

[9] Copyright © Arthur Wind & Fyre Music Corporation Ltd, 2019

'Ohhhhhhhh . . .

I'm a happy carrot

I'm pleased as punch

Perfect for a light snack

Or having with your lunch

I'm a cheerful carrot

And I'm perfectly orange

The only thing that rhymes with that

Is something called a sporange.

I'm delicious and nutritious

Extremely hard and crunchy

Much nicer than this potato

Who really wants to punch me!'

Dylan finished with another awkward bow. Charlie then had to pretend to punch Dylan. He did this with perhaps more gusto than they had rehearsed before.

Then it was time for Charlie's 'Sad Potato'[10] song.

He opened his mouth to sing, but nothing came out. He froze.

He couldn't remember the words.

His mouth went dry.

Mr Wind and Ms Fyre stared at Charlie, waiting.

[10] Copyright © Arthur Wind & Fyre Music Corporation Ltd, 2019

Charlie needed a wee and poo all of a sudden.

And then, from nowhere, the words began tumbling out of him:

'Ohhhhhhhhh . . .
I'm a sad potato
I'm an unhappy spud
I'm stuck underground
And I'm covered in mud!

Oh, I'm a glum potato
I'm a tuber with a frown
Growing the wrong way up
Cos I'm planted upside down.
A sad potato's a bad potato
And I really shouldn't whine
But I've got roots growing
Where the sun don't shine.'

He'd done it! He got through the song without

changing! Charlie turned round to Dylan, who was looking at him, waiting. And then, a smile creeping on his face, Dylan mouthed one word at Charlie:

Change!

Charlie felt his eye begin to twitch.

And then the other eye began to twitch. He felt hot. He felt full of static.

Charlie was changing. Dylan had done it.

Mr Wind and Ms Fyre sat blinking up at Charlie, waiting for him to say his final line and leave the stage.

Charlie decided that not bothering with the final line and leaving the stage as swiftly as possible was an excellent idea.

He ran.

He jumped off the stage, ran through the hall, and burst out the doors, running straight into a corridor full of chattering children.

He had to get away from them.

His body was now spitting and fizzing with electricity.

Any second now he'd change.

He legged it down the corridor, his body full of fire. Footsteps were pounding behind him. Charlie turned and saw Dylan giving chase, a determined look on his face.

Charlie flew round a corner into an empty corridor and felt himself shrinking as he ran.

And he kept shrinking.

And kept shrinking.

The corridor suddenly seemed unimaginably huge.

He was tiny and yet still shrinking.

His skin was gone; his body now covered in interlocking brown scales. Charlie had changed into – well, he had no idea what he'd changed into but it was absolutely minuscule.

At that moment Dylan burst round the corner . . .

Into an empty corridor.

It wasn't completely empty, of course. Charlie was there – but he was now about the size of a grain of rice, and Dylan obviously couldn't see him.

Dylan stalked down the corridor, looking around suspiciously.

He stepped slowly over Charlie without spotting him.

Dylan was the size of a skyscraper, bigger, in fact, his body stretching off into the distance, towards a ceiling that looked to Charlie as far away and immense as the sky. Dylan's feet were the size of football pitches, and they slapped down on the floor, nearly squashing him.

Charlie remained totally still, terrified of getting crushed by the giant shoes as Dylan walked past.

Suddenly the lunch bell rang. Charlie remembered with a sickening jolt that the corridor he was in led directly to the school cafe. And that meant it was about to be swamped with –

There was the sound of feet – lots and lots of feet – all charging towards the cafe. And, more to the point, charging towards Charlie.

Now, Charlie had been scared in his life before, but nothing – NOTHING – could have prepared him for the sight of an army of mountain-sized children thundering towards him with marathon-length strides.

I'm definitely going to get squashed, Charlie thought, terror-stricken.

He had to somehow get out of the way.

Maybe he could try jumping.

Charlie jumped.

And he jumped higher and further and faster than he could have believed possible. He was Superman, soaring through the air with such ease he felt like he was flying again.

And as he made his second jump, he realized exactly what he was.

Charlie was a flea.

He jumped in between the legs of the children, hopping to and fro, exhilarated by his extraordinary new-found gymnastic ability.

He still had to get out of the corridor, though, and quickly. If he changed back to his usual self here, he'd be seen by everybody. And that wouldn't be good *at all*.

Charlie began hopping from kid to kid. He jumped upwards, from legs to arms, until finally he landed on the head of a tall Year Five girl,

and nestled in her hair. From here Charlie had a perfect vantage point. He had covered a lot of ground. He was nearly at the end of the corridor. If he could make it into a classroom, chances were it would be empty because it was lunchtime, and hopefully he'd change back quickly without being seen.

He saw the face of the person next to the girl he was riding – it was Teddy, Dylan's best friend.

Even though it would cost him time, Charlie couldn't resist. He jumped on to Teddy's shoulder and then up to his neck. And as hard as he could he took a great big bite.

But Charlie had forgotten for a moment why fleas bite. Before he knew it he was sucking Teddy's blood. With a heave of disgust he stopped biting and tried spitting the blood out. Although still disgusted, he was happy in the knowledge that Teddy would have a nasty, itchy fleabite.

He began hopping from head to head across the sea of children that stretched out in front of him.

Boing! On to Francis from 3P's curly hair.

Boing! On to Ava from 4R's long plaited hair.

Boing! On to James from 2S's short spiky hair.

And so he bounced and hopped all the way to the end of the corridor.

The first classroom he came to – Class 2R – he crawled under the door into what seemed to be a mercifully silent classroom. It was so huge and he was so tiny that he couldn't possibly see the whole of it, but it seemed like the coast was clear.

He remained still and waited. And waited.

And waited.

And then, with a surge of relief, he felt the change coming back. His arms, hair, his skin, all returned. Up he grew, and before he knew it he was back to plain old Charlie McGuffin and standing in a silent room.

'Hello, Charlie. I guessed you might end up in here.'

Charlie swung round.

Dylan was standing behind him at the back of the room. And he was holding a phone pointed straight at Charlie.

'Say hello to the camera, Charlie. Give us a wave. I've been recording the whole show. The whole disgusting sight of you changing from a tiny bug back to Charlie.'

Charlie gulped.

'Give me the phone, Dylan.'

'Oh no,' Dylan said with a cackle. 'Not a chance. We're going to be famous, you and I. We don't have to wait for you to change in front of everyone at the play: this exclusive footage is going to go viral. Now I get to be rich, and you're finished, and out of this school for good.'

'Please, Dylan. Just give it to me.'

'Ha, OK, yeah, forget the whole plan, here you go, take the phone. NOT. I'm not an idiot, Charlie.'

'That's debatable.'

'Calling me names is not going to help you, Charlie. In fact, nothing will. Goodbye, Charlie McGuffin.'

And with that Dylan slipped the phone into his pocket and walked out of the classroom.

Charlie chased him into the corridor, calling after him.

Dylan simply ignored him.

That was it then. Charlie was finished.

Out of nowhere a child-sized stick of broccoli steamrollered round the corner and barrelled straight into Dylan, who was knocked backwards on to his bottom.

It was Wogan, closely followed by Flora and Mohsen.

Dylan picked himself up, and dusted himself down.

'Watch where you're going, you idiots!' he seethed, and stormed off down the corridor.

'What's his problem?' asked Wogan, panting. 'And where've you been? We've been looking all over for you since you bolted from the rehearsal. What happened?'

'Changed again, didn't I?'

'No way! What to this time?'

'A flea,' replied Charlie.

'Whoa! No wonder you had to *flee* so quickly,' Mohsen said, grinning at his own joke.

Flora and Charlie glared at Mohsen. Wogan looked confused.

'This is not the time for jokes, Mohsen,' said Flora.

'Look, that's not important,' said Charlie. 'I've got more problems to worry about. I'm in big trouble.'

'Bigger than usual?' said Mohsen.

'The biggest. Dylan followed me and recorded me changing back. He said he's going to show it to the world. So basically I'm a dead man unless we can somehow get Dylan's phone from him before he does anything with the video.'

'You mean this phone?' said Flora.

The three boys looked at Flora, who was holding a phone.

'Yes,' said Charlie. 'It's exactly like that phone.'

'That's because this *is* Dylan's phone,' said Flora, blinking.

'Look, Flora, this isn't the time for any more of your ridiculous –'

'He dropped it,' Flora interrupted. 'When Wogan bumped into him and he fell over.'

'You're . . . You're kidding?!' said Charlie, mouth flapping like a dying fish.

'I saw it fly out of his pocket. So I picked it up. I was about to give it back to him but he was rude so I sort of accidentally kept hold of it. So you can just delete the video and give it him straight back.'

'Flora,' gasped Charlie. 'You are an actual proper real-life lifesaver.' Charlie took the phone off Flora and deleted the video. Without thinking, he grinned at her and said, 'I could kiss you.'

Flora blushed as soon as he said that. And Charlie blushed right back.

CHAPTER 9

Handing the phone back to Dylan was easily the highlight of Charlie's week. Dylan's face when he saw the video had been deleted was an image Charlie would not forget in a long time: it was somewhere between bright red and purple, a beautiful mixture of disbelief and fury.

Once that fun was over, though, Charlie and his friends' minds all turned back to the problem in hand: how to stop Charlie turning into an animal before the school play arrived. It wasn't until the next day that Flora devised the experiment that would test her latest theory – that stress was causing him to change. Changing into a flea during the rehearsal was more evidence, but Flora had to be certain. She needed final, absolute proof. And Flora revealed to Charlie exactly how they were going to get it while they were all playing tennis. They had just had a long rally and stopped for a breather.

'I think I've worked it out. It came to me this morning. But you're not going to like it.'

'What a surprise,' said Charlie.

'No. You really won't,' said Mohsen.

'I'm sure I won't,' said Charlie.

'No. You REALLY, REALLY won't. You're going to hate it,' said Wogan.

'Oh, just tell me! It can't be that bad.'

'Right,' said Flora. 'Right. OK. Here goes. Here's what I want you to do. I'm about to tell you what you should do. OK. You ready?'

'Yes! Just tell me! It can't be *that* bad!'

It *was* that bad. Worse, in fact.

'OK then,' Flora said. 'What you need to do

is . . .' She took a deep breath. 'Break into Ms Fyre's office and shave her monkey.'

Now, out of context that is a pretty weird sentence. So, let's answer some of your questions straight away and then we'll get right back to the story.

l. Josh, nine, from Whitstable asks: 'Does Ms Fyre really have an actual live monkey in her office?' *It would be awesome if Ms Fyre really did have an actual monkey in her office, but that would be ridiculous. This is a very serious book about a boy who can change into animals and shoot ropes out of his butt and has numerous pigeons with terrible French accents fall in love with him. So, no, of course it isn't a* real *monkey in her office. Silly question, Josh from Whitstable. I know you're only nine, but your parents must be very disappointed in you. Frankly we're all a little disappointed in you.*

2. 'So, in that case, what is the monkey then?' asks Jennifer, eight, from Ballina, County Mayo in Ireland. *Excellent question, Jennifer. You're clearly a smart cookie. Well, let me tell you what the monkey is. It's a huge stuffed cuddly toy monkey. It's as big as you, Jennifer. It's that big.*

3. 'Where did this monkey come from?' asks Josh, nine, from Whitstable. *OK, Josh. That's a much better question. You've taken the criticism on board. You've pulled your socks up. I'm impressed with your attitude, Josh. Great work.*

4. 'You didn't answer my question,' says Josh, nine, from Whitstable. *Good point, Josh. The answer to the question is nobody really knows. Some say Mr Wind was seen*

*walking away from the 'hook-a-duck' stall
at the local fair, carrying the monkey under
his arm, in the very same week it appeared
in Ms Fyre's office, but that's just a rumour.*

5. 'How on earth is Charlie supposed to break into Ms Fyre's office and shave the monkey? And what will he use to actually shave the monkey?' ask Mr (forty-eight) and Mrs (forty-six) Lloyd from Wimbledon. *Well, Mr and Mrs Lloyd from Wimbledon, you will just have to wait and find out. That's the plot. All will be revealed shortly. Just be patient.*

6. 'Isn't breaking into an office and shaving somebody's toy monkey illegal?' asks Josh, nine, from Whitstable. *Look, Josh. You've* *already asked two questions, OK? And you've just undone all the good work you did with your second question. Don't take this story too seriously. This is a ridiculous book about a boy who can change into animals and shoot ropes out of his butt and has numerous pigeons with terrible French accents fall in love with him. So let's just forget any legal implications, yes? Agreed, Josh? Good. OK. Let's get back to the story. No more interruptions, please.*

'Let me get this right. You want me to break into Ms Fyre's office and shave her monkey?' asked Charlie incredulously.

Flora nodded. 'That's right.'

'I think we need to get a doctor to see you. You've finally lost it. Properly this time.'

'I have not. It's the only way to know for certain.'

'It's the only way to get me in detention until I'm eighteen AND hung upside down by my toes by my parents until I leave home.'

'Charlie, listen. We need to know for *absolute* certain what causes you to change before we can work out how to stop it. And we've only got six days until the school play.'

'Well, you can't argue with that,' said Wogan.

'I can. And I am.' Charlie crossed his arms.

'Well, OK, you can. But she's right.'

The four of them stood in silence for a moment. Wogan started boinging a ball in the air with his racquet.

'Come on, Charlie. It'll be something you'll never forget as long as you live,' Flora said.

Charlie stared at Flora for the longest time, then exploded.

'GAAAAAAH OK I'LL DO IT I'LL DO IT GAAAAAHHH!'

Flora beamed.

'Oh, Charlie! You're doing the right thing. Science will thank you. You're like Neil Armstrong taking a giant leap for mankind.'

'I can't believe I am agreeing to one of your RIDICULOUS plans AGAIN. I must have really lost it this time.'

'You haven't lost it. You're brave,' said Flora.

'Well, let's be honest, he's lost it a bit. I mean, breaking into Miss Fyre's office? Shaving her monkey? It's certain death,' said Wogan helpfully.

'Wogan!' said Flora, glaring at Wogan. 'That is actually not helpful. At all.'

'OK. So many questions. Where to begin? First question: how am I going to shave the monkey?'

'Don't worry. I have it all planned out. Does your dad use an electric shaver?'

'Yes,' replied Charlie.

'Well, there you go then. You just borrow your dad's electric shaver on the day.'[11]

'Oh. That simple.'

'Yes, exactly. That simple.'

'And when do we do it?'

'We just watch for her leaving her office for lunch. Then you sneak in, shave the monkey, sneak out again. Simple.'

'Yeah. Simple,' said Charlie, who thought it sounded about as simple as doing rocket surgery on a brain scientist. 'And what happens if I get caught?'

---

[11] You see, I told you you'd find out, Mr and Mrs Lloyd.

'You *won't* get caught. We'll keep watch. Trust me.'

'Yes. Trust you. That's the problem.'

'You do *trust* me, don't you, Charlie?' said Flora.

'Absolutely. One hundred per cent,' said Charlie, who right at that moment trusted Flora about as far as he could throw her.[12] 'So when do we do this?'

'Tomorrow,' said Flora with a glint in her eye. 'Argh!' she shouted suddenly, rubbing her face.

'What?' asked Charlie.

'I think I've got a glint stuck in my eye,' said Flora. 'It must have just flown in.'

'Do you want us to take you to the toilet?' asked Wogan with some concern. 'If you splash

---

[12] Charlie could throw Flora approximately 26 centimetres. So Charlie trusted Flora about 26 centimetres, which does not make any sense at all when you think about it. Just take from this that Charlie doesn't trust Flora very much, and let's just move on. But you should also know that Charlie has never actually attempted to throw Flora, who has a blue belt in karate and would probably beat him up if he did.

water on your eye, it might come out.'

'Thanks, Wogan. Yes, please. It's quite sore,' said Flora, still rubbing her eye.

'OK, see you later, Charlie,' said Wogan.

'See you in a bit, Charlie,' said Mohsen.

And with that, Wogan, Mohsen and Flora walked off, leaving Charlie standing there with thoughts of bald monkeys and certain doom swirling round his head.

CHAPTER 10

Wogan, Mohsen, Flora and Charlie were skulking. They had just rushed out of lunch, and were hanging round in the corridor near Ms Fyre's office. Bulging in Charlie's pocket was his dad's electric shaver, which he had sneaked into his bag that morning. If he got it back in the bathroom as soon as he got home, his dad would never know.

The minutes ticked by as they nervously waited for Ms Fyre to leave her office.

Finally the door swung open, and Ms Fyre marched out towards the school cafe.

'OK, people! Take your positions!' whispered Flora dramatically.

Wogan quickly chased after Ms Fyre. He positioned himself in the next corridor, so he had the perfect view of her in the canteen, where she would soon be holding a tray and choosing her lunch. If Ms Fyre did anything, Wogan would be able to warn Mohsen, who was standing at the corner, where he could see both Wogan and Flora, who was standing outside Ms Fyre's office with Charlie. Wogan gave Mohsen the thumbs up, and Mohsen turned and gave Flora

the thumbs up.

'OK. It's time. Good luck, Charlie McGuffin,' said Flora.

There was something nagging in the back of Charlie's mind, but he dismissed it. The plan was ready. It was now or never.

He nodded solemnly to Flora and took one last look up and down the corridor to make sure the coast was clear. He placed his hand on the handle, swallowed and, quick as a flash, sneaked into the office.

The minute the door closed behind him he realized what had been nagging him. He was desperate for a wee. He opened the door again.

'Flora!'

'What do you want? Get back in there!' Flora asked.

'I'm busting for a wee!'

'Charlie, we don't have time!' Flora said,

slapping her forehead. 'Get back in there and shave monkey! Ms Fyre could be back any moment. You can have a wee after!'

'OK, OK. I'm going in.'

Reluctantly Charlie crept back into the office and tried to forget about the wee.

He closed the door of the office behind him, and tiptoed into the stuffy silence. It was a pretty ordinary office, apart from Ms Fyre's prize orchids, which lined the windowsill. And of course, sitting there like a giant stuffed monkey on a bookshelf sat the giant monkey on top of the bookshelf. There was no way Charlie could reach it, so he pulled Ms Fyre's swivel chair over and began to climb on it.

Meanwhile, Wogan, who was spying on Ms Fyre, was the first person to realize that things were about to go wrong. Horribly, horribly wrong. He watched in horror as Ms Fyre began patting her pockets as if she'd lost something, tutted, and began walking towards Wogan, who froze in terror, his brain crashing. Fortunately his body snapped into action. He began frantically waving at Mohsen.

Unfortunately, just at that precise moment, Mohsen had found a particularly well-lodged bogey and was giving that his full attention rather than the frantically waving Wogan. Wogan realized that no matter how much he waved, Mohsen was just not going to see him. Ms Fyre was already nearly on top of him, so Wogan made a decision and began running towards Mohsen.

'She's coming!' Wogan panted.

'What?' said Mohsen, one finger still deeply embedded in his left nostril.

'Fyre's coming! Look!'

A look of horror spread across

Mohsen's face as he saw Ms Fyre striding back towards her office. Immediately he swung round and began waving madly at Flora.

Flora, fortunately, was keeping good watch. Her face paling when she saw Mohsen's panicked waving, she quickly gave three knocks on the office door. That was the agreed signal for Charlie to hide. They couldn't risk Charlie leaving the office in case he was seen, so they had agreed that if Ms Fyre returned early that Charlie would hide and Flora would try to delay her to give Charlie longer to get himself hidden.

When Charlie heard Flora's three sharp knocks his heart nearly fell out of his bum.

He jumped down off the swivel chair, and looked round in blind panic. He dived down under the desk and curled up into a ball. Then, with a shock of fear, he realized that he had left the chair by the bookcase, and not by the desk where it belonged. He scrambled out, and began pulling the chair backwards when he heard the voice of Flora, suddenly, loud, right outside the door.

'Oh, hi, Ms Fyre.'

'Good afternoon, child. Out of my way and allow me to enter my office.' Ms Fyre's cut-glass voice cut through the closed door.

'But . . . how are you, Ms Fyre?'

'I'm perfectly adequate, thank you, now if you would move out of the way –'

'Ms Fyre, can I just say you're looking really lovely today? The way the sun is shining through the window on to your head, it makes your hair look beautiful, like a great big bush caught fire.'

Charlie crawled backwards under the desk, dragging the chair with him.

'Hmm. Why, thank you, I suppose. Now out of my way, child.'

'But, Ms Fyre, can I just show you, I've got this strange rash –'

'Then go to the nurse, child. Out. Of. My.

Way. Now!'

Just as Charlie got in position, curled tightly up under the desk, the office door opened. Charlie stopped breathing, terrified the noise would give him away.

Ms Fyre walked in. Charlie could see her feet, long toenails poking out of the front of her open-toed sandals. If Charlie didn't know better, he'd swear the toenails were chewed.

Charlie kept his breath held. In a second he knew the breath would escape in a loud gasp. His heart was pounding. He *really* needed that wee now.

From her desk Ms Fyre picked up something that jangled suspiciously like a set of keys, put it in her pocket and went to the door.

Without Charlie or Flora seeing, she popped a little button on the handle, walked out of the office and closed the door behind her.

Charlie let out a gasp of relief.

He really shouldn't have done. He certainly *wouldn't* have done if he had known that the tiny button Ms Fyre had pressed had just sealed his fate.

Because that button had caused the door to lock automatically behind Ms Fyre. It could now only be opened with a key. A key that nestled in Ms Fyre's jacket pocket.

But Charlie didn't know that as he sprang out from under the desk, dragged the chair over to the bookshelf again and pulled the monkey down. He took out his father's electric shaver, turned it on and began shaving the monkey. The shaver seemed deafeningly loud in the silence of Ms Fyre's office.

Black tufts of hair drifted and fell at his feet.

It was taking longer than he'd thought. It was a BIG monkey and the shaver could only do so much. The seconds ticked by. The shaver hummed and black fur fell. Soon the monkey was half shaved. For the briefest moment guilt rippled through him – this was somebody's cuddly toy he was destroying after all. But it was for science, he reminded himself. And he was desperate.

The pain in his bladder was getting worse. He had to hurry up. On he shaved, a small

mountain of fur growing at his feet. The monkey was three quarters shaved now. There was just its head and bum left to do.

It was going to be close. The pain was getting unbearable.

The head was done. Just the hairy bum left.

The bald monkey was now looking very weird indeed, like a pale, skinny alien. With a furry bum.

The final few tufts fell away. Finished! Charlie jumped back on to the chair and threw the bald, alien monkey-creature back on to the bookshelf. He quickly swept up the hair and threw it into the bin. He was going to wet himself if he didn't get out of the office fast. He pushed the chair back to the desk and ran to the door.

He tried the handle.

It didn't open.

He tried pulling harder.

It was completely stuck.

Charlie was locked in Ms Fyre's office. He was a prisoner.

There was a small square window in the door, which he could just reach by standing on tiptoes. He peeped out and saw Flora. He knocked on the window.

'Flora! Help!' Charlie whisper-shouted. 'It's locked!'

'What?' Flora whisper-shouted back. 'I can't hear you!' She pointed to her ears and shook her head.

'Gah!' cried Charlie, frustrated. 'I'm stuck and I'm about to wee in my pants!'

'You're a duck and you've got bikini pants?!' Flora replied through the window, looking very confused. 'Are you feeling all right, Charlie?'

'No!' Charlie hissed, a little louder. 'I'm stuck! **I'M LOCKED IN!**'

The realization of Charlie's dire situation hit

Flora like a slap in the face with a heavy simile.

She gasped. 'You're locked in?' She rattled the door handle, pulling it frantically. It didn't budge.

Charlie looked at Flora mournfully through the window. She looked back, her face a mixture of apology and pity and desperation.

'What can I do?' Charlie mouthed, panic in his face. 'The wee is about to come!'

'Do it in the orchids!' Flora shouted in a flash of inspiration.

'What? I can't!'

'You can! Wee in the flowerpots! Ms Fyre will never notice!' Flora urged.

Charlie knew right then he had no choice. The wee was coming.

'OH GOD, OK, OK! I'M GOING TO!'

He rushed over to the orchids, closed his eyes and prayed that Ms Fyre wouldn't burst in on him now.

He started weeing into the nearest orchid.

The pain immediately turned into relief as he started filling the pot.

Very quickly, though, the pot filled and, with a panicky hop, Charlie had to jiggle over to the next orchid pot and continue his wee into that.

By the time he had finished Charlie had filled four flowerpots.

But Charlie didn't care. Charlie felt *fantastic*. For a few short seconds.

Then he remembered his hideous situation.

He was imprisoned in Ms Fyre's office with a shaved monkey, an electric shaver, a binful of black fur and four orchid pots brimming with wee.

He checked the windows. They only opened right at the top and there was no way he could climb up. He tried the door again – out of wild desperation – but it was still completely locked, no matter how hard he rattled the handle.

He looked around wildly. There *had* to be a way out of there.

There wasn't.

Suddenly there came three knocks on the door. Flora's stricken face was at the window. She mouthed two simple, clear words.

'She's coming.'

Charlie felt his world crumbling.

And then Flora followed with two more words:

'I'm sorry.'

Charlie understood what that meant. They'd discussed it before the mission had begun. If things got really bad, Flora had to leave. She had to save herself. He didn't blame her. He understood. There was no reason why she should let herself get caught.

Charlie, on the other hand, was finished. Done for.

There was no escape.

He slumped to the floor and awaited his fate. He'd get excluded, definitely. Expelled, almost certainly. His mum and dad would go absolutely completely one hundred per cent bananas – and with his brother's scan in a few days this was the last thing they needed. He'd get grounded forever. He'd lose all PS4 and Netflix privileges.

His life wouldn't be worth living. The only silver lining was that he knew when his brother found out that this story would definitely put a smile on his face.

Knowing it was pointless, Charlie crawled back under the desk, to the only hiding place in the office, and curled into a tight ball.

A key rattled in the door.

Charlie scrunched up his eyes and his mind crossed the border from wretchedness into total desolation.

The lock clicked.

It was the end for Charlie.

And then he felt it. Electricity shooting through his body. His very being buzzing with jolts of fiery energy.

His body squeezing.

His arms disappearing.

His legs disappearing.

His hair disappearing.

His body stretching, lengthening. Charlie's tongue growing. His skin turning green and brown, scales appearing.

The door opened. Footsteps.

He'd changed, and he knew immediately what he'd changed into. His tongue flickered out of his mouth and he could taste the air; he could taste the smell of Ms Fyre in the office.

Ms Fyre stood stock-still in the centre of her office and sniffed.

She sniffed again. Then she began to sniff around the office, getting closer, closer, closer to the orchids.

She took one final sniff, and saw the orchid pots overflowing with wee.

She gasped, her hand fluttering round her mouth. 'I don't believe it!'

She started prowling around the office, her beady eyes scanning, until they landed on the bald monkey sitting on her bookshelf.

She gave a cry of dismay and pulled the monkey down.

'Geoffrey! What have they done to you? How could they be –'

Ms Fyre stopped in her tracks.

'Wait a moment,' she said to herself. 'The door was locked. That means whoever did this is still here . . . And there is only one place they can be . . .'

She strode over to her desk, squatted down . . .

And screamed.

'SNAKE!!!!!'

Ms Fyre fell backwards on to her bum and screamed again.

'THERE'S A SNAKE IN MY OFFICE!'

She leaped up and ran out, slamming the door behind her and locking it again.

The situation was grim.

Charlie was a snake. He was STILL locked in Ms Fyre's office. And in no time at all he would be caught red-handed.[13]

[13] Or no-handed, technically, because snakes don't have hands.

CHAPTER 11

Charlie knew he only had a matter of moments before Ms Fyre returned with help. He had to think fast.

He had no time to dwell on the extraordinary feeling of being a snake. No time to appreciate his new long, lithe muscular body. His brain was being overloaded with a barrage of new information. Every time his forked tongue flickered out of his mouth he could taste the smell of Ms Fyre's sweat lingering in the room, and he could feel through his stomach the receding footsteps of the head teacher sprinting down the corridor.

He slithered around the carpeted floor of the

office, trying to find a suitable escape hole. Nothing. He arched his head up and spied something that made his snake heart burst with hope: an air vent high up in the corner of the room.

He zigzagged across the room, and began stretching his long body to try to reach the vent. As much as he could stretch, though, he couldn't quite get there.

Well, then, I'll just have to go the long way around, Charlie thought.

He slithered over to the bookcase and zipped up the shelves all the way to the top. He could feel the vibrations of more footsteps, lots of them, pounding down the corridor towards the office.

The teachers were coming, and at top speed.

From the top of the bookcase he was able to slide over to the curtain rail and then along it.

From there he might just be able to reach the air vent.

He heard the sound of a key in the door and loud voices outside clamouring to get in.

Charlie stretched his long body across the corner of the room, and his head was just able to reach the air vent. His tongue flickered involuntarily – he could taste dust and spiders and stale air. He started sliding into the blackness.

He felt Ms Fyre's door crash open and footsteps tumble in to the office just as the end of his tail disappeared into the vent.

'Find it!'

'Where is it?'

'Are you absolutely *sure* it was a *snake*, Ms Fyre?'

The voices echoed behind Charlie as he slid through the dark shaft that linked the office to – well, Charlie actually had no idea where he was going. All he knew and cared about was that he was free from the office. And didn't need a wee.

He also knew that he really did NOT want to change back while he was still in the shaft. That would be beyond awful. The consequences of suddenly expanding into a full-size Charlie in a space that certainly couldn't fit a full-size Charlie would be very messy indeed.

So he slithered as fast as he could down the tiny passage, until he came to the next vent. He could smell it was a toilet even before he poked his head through the grille. He slid straight through the gap into a brightly lit, and fortunately empty, toilet. He slithered straight down the wall into an empty cubicle, and tried to take stock of his situation.

If he could just wait it out, he would change back to Charlie and everything would be OK. He couldn't wait to tell the others: Flora was

right. She was absolutely right about everything – him changing *was* related to stress. *She should definitely be a scientist,* Charlie thought. And he couldn't wait to tell Flora about his latest adventure, changing into a snake and escaping from the rampaging teachers. She might, Charlie hoped, think that he had been rather brave.

But first he had to change back. And as long as nobody came into the toilet, Charlie thought, he'd be fine.

Charlie really shouldn't have thought that last thought.

Because, obviously, approximately one nanosecond after he thought it, the toilet door opened and to Charlie's horror a bunch of girls stampeded in, chattering and giggling. He was in the *girls'* toilet! If he had a hand or a forehead, he would have slapped the latter with the former.[14] He tried to groan, and immediately discovered that when a snake attempts to groan it comes out as a long hiss.

Now, if you want to silence a group of loud, chattering girls in a school toilet, pretty much the quickest way to do it is to:

1. Be a snake, and

2. Hiss loudly from one of the toilet cubicles.

[14] There is much discussion among scientists whether snakes have foreheads. One scientist has even argued that a snake's body is essentially one long forehead, but he has been shunned by all the other snakeologists for his barmy theories, and he is now banned from coming to the Annual Snakeologists' Christmas Party, which is sad and unfair but quite understandable.

There is no discussion among scientists whether snakes have hands.

And that's exactly what happened – the girls immediately froze in stunned silence. Then, in unison, they all turned their heads to the cubicle from which the hiss had come.

Slowly, ever so slowly, all holding their breath, the girls edged their way to the cubicle door. The bravest, a girl called Molly (who would one day become the first person to climb Mount Everest while carrying a miniature llama strapped to her back – do NOT ask why), stepped towards the door. With just the briefest moment of hesitation she placed one hand on the door, and pushed it open.

And there, coiled on the floor of the toilet, was to their utter horror a spectacular two-metre-long reticulated python. Or Charlie the Snake as we know him.

The silence broke with the sound of four girls screaming at the very top of their voices, which, as everybody knows, is the loudest sound on the planet.

The vibration of the scream hit Charlie like a high-speed brick wall, if brick walls could travel at high speed (and we should all be glad they can't). It sent him into a frenzied panic, and he began twisting and writhing, which made the girls scream even louder. And through the cloud of panic he realized there was only one way out.

Charlie took a deep breath and slid over the edge of the toilet bowl and down into the water. Yes – down into the wee-wee water. And he started swimming as fast as he could down the toilet and through the U-bend and then into the pipes. As he swam he decided that he would probably leave this part of the story out when telling Mohsen, Wogan and Flora about his time as a snake. *I mean, there's no need for them to know* all *the details*, he thought as he swam past a small poo.

Charlie was quickly running out of breath. But ahead of him was a pipe that headed upwards, and 'up' hopefully meant 'air'. His lungs bursting, he swam hard, darting upwards like an arrow towards a glimmering crescent of light.

He burst out of the water and hit something soft.

Something pink.

Something fleshy.

Now, meanwhile, Charlie's arch-nemesis Dylan had been minding his own business.

Minding his own business sitting on a toilet.

And then the last thing Dylan ever dreamed would happen DID happen.

A two-metre-long reticulated python sprang out of the toilet that Dylan was sitting on and hit him right on the bum.

'Yeeeoooow!'

Dylan leaped off the toilet as if it was

electrified. He clung to the top of the cubicle door, his pants round his ankles, his legs flapping and flailing. But as soon as he turned his head and saw what had burst out of the toilet, he knew. He just *knew* it had to be Charlie.

Charlie, meanwhile, couldn't believe his awful luck. Of all the bums to bump head-first into, it had to be Dylan's. He slithered out of the toilet, glistening wet and gasping, then underneath the flailing figure of Dylan and the cubicle door into the bathroom. Dylan jumped down, pulled his pants up and dived out of the door after Charlie. He sprang out into the bathroom and, while keeping his eyes on Charlie, knelt down and carefully opened his school bag as wide as he could.

And then he began to creep closer to Charlie, arms spread-eagled.

Charlie realized what Dylan was trying to do

a split second too late. He tried darting past him, but Dylan dived on the floor and grabbed him. Charlie was strong and able to use all the muscles in his long body, but Dylan was lying on top of him and he couldn't get away. Dylan grabbed him by the neck and Charlie couldn't escape. His head was being forced into the dark of Dylan's school bag, and Charlie thought he would puke at the smell of squashed banana and smelly socks. As much as he struggled, Dylan was managing to push him into the bag centimetre by centimetre.

The familiar rush of electricity through his body couldn't have come at a better time. Charlie felt it, the fire, along the whole length of his body, but a fire trapped, contained but roaring. He could feel his limbs growing back, his hair springing out, hands, nails and all his human bits and pieces returning.

He felt Dylan get knocked backwards on to the floor.

And then, with a crash, Mr Wind burst through the bathroom door.

What Mr Wind saw when he charged into the lavatories was:

1. Dylan, panting, lying on his back on the floor.

2. Another boy, as yet unidentified, but who we know to be Charlie, also lying on the floor in a soaking wet uniform with his head stuck inside a school bag.

'WHAT IS THE MEANING OF THIS?!' Mr Wind shouted. **'TAKE THAT BAG OFF YOUR HEAD IMMEDIATELY, BOY.'**

Charlie sheepishly took the bag off his head. He blinked in the light. The smell of the toilet was a relief after the stench of Dylan's bag.

'Now can someone explain exactly what is going on here? Why are you soaking wet, McGuffin? And why on earth did you have a bag on your head?' He glared at Dylan, clearly suspicious. Dylan's track record as a bully was well known. 'Is this your doing, boy?'

'No, Mr Wind, sir.' Dylan did his best to look innocent, but he wasn't very convincing and just looked constipated.

'Well?' Mr Wind eyed Charlie beadily. 'Attacked, were you? Bog-washing was it, McGuffin?'

I could get him in SO much trouble, Charlie

thought. *All I have to do is tell . . .*

Dylan looked at Charlie with a mixture of defiance and resignation. But both were surprised at the words that actually did fall out of Charlie's mouth.

'No, sir. Dylan had nothing to do with it. It was an accident.'

Charlie wasn't entirely sure why he said that, but he felt good saying it. Like it was the right thing to do.

Dylan's eyes were saucers.

Mr Wind narrow-eyed Charlie.

'An accident? What sort of accident?' Mr Wind asked in a voice dripping with suspicion.

'I fell, sir. Into the toilet. And Dylan helped me out, sir.'

'You fell? Into the toilet?' Mr Wind said in disbelief.

'Yes, sir,' both boys said in unison.

'But . . . How do you fall into a toilet?'

'Tripped, sir,' Charlie replied without hesitation.

'Tripped,' Mr Wind said, shaking his head, clearly not believing a word of it. 'Well, how did you get the bag on your head then?'

Charlie and Dylan looked at each other. Charlie didn't have a clue what to say. How was he going to explain this away?

'He was helping me, sir. To see if my bag smelled funny,' Dylan blurted out.

'So he trips and falls into the toilet and then the first thing you do is ask him to check your bag to see if it smells funny?' Mr Wind repeated, still clearly not believing a word of what they were saying.

'Yes, sir.' Charlie and Dylan both nodded their heads vigorously.

'And it did smell funny, sir. Bananas and sweaty socks,' Charlie added.

Mr Wind shook his head.

'What utter balderdash. A huge pile of piffle and bunkum . . .'

Charlie and Dylan looked at each other mystified.

'Balder*what*, sir?' Charlie asked.

'Your story. Pure hogwash. Ludicrous. Well, what do I care? I've got far more important things to be dealing with, what with snakes on the loose.'

'Snakes, sir?' said Charlie innocently. 'On the loose? In school? Are you *sure*?'

'*Yes, I'm sure!* Poor Ms Fyre has had the fright of her life. And somebody around here has to protect her. Well, just dry yourself off then, boy. I don't suppose either of you have seen a snake in here, have you?' Mr Wind eyed them suspiciously.

'No, sir,' they both said quick as a flash.

'Hmm. Well, get out of here then.' Mr Wind pointed to the door. 'Snakes are dangerous creatures. A snake hunt is only for adults. *Brave* adults.'

Both Dylan and Charlie couldn't help but smile as they shut the toilet door behind them. They were silent for a few moments as they walked along the corridor.

'Why didn't you . . .?' Dylan left the question hanging.

'I don't know,' replied Charlie.

'Well – thanks,' Dylan said gruffly. 'And anyway,' he continued, 'when you reappeared, yeah? Where did your clothes come from?'

'What?' asked Charlie.

'Well, OK, it's one thing you turning from a human into an animal and back again because you are some sort of genetic freak. There's some scientific logic there. I understand that. But your clothes disappearing and then reappearing? How does that happen? Is that magic? I really hope there is some sort of reasonable and satisfactory explanation for this so we aren't left with some great big giant obvious plot hole at the end of our epic battle of wits,' Dylan said.

'Oh, don't worry,' Charlie replied. 'I am absolutely certain that there is a clear and logical reason why my clothes disappear and reappear as if by magic.'[15]

'And,' Charlie continued. 'There definitely won't be some great big giant obvious plot hole at the end of our epic battle of wits.'[16]

[15] There wasn't.

[16] There will be.

'So are you nervous about the play?' Charlie asked, wary of a friendly conversation with Dylan.

'Not at all,' said Dylan. 'I know my lines. And I know my "Happy Carrot" song. And I can't wait to see you turn into an animal in front of the whole school and sent to a freak show.'

Charlie grimaced. Each time he trusted Dylan, Dylan threw it back in his face.

'You don't have to be nasty, you know. You could try being nice.'

'Oh, nice is so boring! Who wants to be nice? I'm the one who injects life and excitement into this world! You *need* me. Have you ever seen a movie without a baddie? No. Exactly. I'm *necessary*. You need me to be like this.'

'You should really talk to the school counsellor, Dylan. I'm not even joking.'

'We're not so different, you and I, Charlie.'

'We actually are. We couldn't be more different.'

'No! We are two sides of the same coin. I'm yin, you're yang. I'm win and you're . . .'

'Wang?' Charlie replied uncertainly.

'Wang?! No! You're lose! Win and *lose*! And lose is what you will do at the school play. Well, Mr McGuffin, I'd like to say it's been a pleasure knowing you. But it hasn't.'

And with that Dylan walked off, laughing to himself.

'Absolute, utter, stark-raving, head-banging weirdo,' Charlie said to the empty corridor.

CHAPTER 12

'I knew it! I knew it! This is brilliant! This is the best news EVER!'

It would be fair to say that Flora was quite pleased when she found out her theory about Charlie changing had been proved correct.

'Well, that's all very well, but it doesn't exactly *help* me,' replied Charlie, glum-faced.

'Of course it helps you! Of course it does!' Flora gripped Charlie's arms, a manic look in her eyes. 'Doesn't it, Mohsen?'

'Yes!' Mohsen answered, a look of mild terror in his eyes.

'Doesn't it, Wogan?' she asked.

'Yes!' Wogan answered, a look of confusion in his eyes.

'It's obvious, Charlie! Now we know *what's* causing you to change, we can work out a way of preventing it! Oh, this is just the breakthrough we needed.'

Flora thumped her palm in triumph.

That's all well and good, Charlie thought, *but what's actually going to* stop *me changing?*

Charlie thought for a little longer, and decided his last thought was actually a pretty good one and should probably be spoken aloud.

'That's all well and good, but what's actually going to *stop* me changing?'

'That's a very sensible and well-thought-out question,' said Flora. 'And I have a plan.' She waggled her eyebrows up and down.

'Does this plan involve putting me in a large amount of danger by any chance? You know, maybe sending me flying down a hill at a million miles an hour? Or shaving the head teacher's most prized possession? Or firing me into space?'

'No. It does not. And if you don't want to hear it, I shan't tell you,' said Flora, crossing her arms.

'I do!' protested Charlie. 'I was only joking. Please. Tell me, Flora. What's your plan?'

'OK, well, the plan is simple. Next time you feel it happening, breathe.'

'Breathe?' asked Charlie.

'Yes,' replied Flora. 'Breathe.'

'Breathe. Brilliant.'

When Charlie said 'brilliant' it really didn't sound like he meant 'brilliant'. It sounded more like 'That is the single worst plan I have heard since Wogan decided not to pack any spare underwear when we went camping to save space in his rucksack for his pet goldfish. And the goldfish bowl.'

'What a marvellous plan,' continued Charlie, 'because my plan was actually *not* to breathe. And then I might die and not have to listen to **ONE OF YOUR AWFUL PLANS EVER AGAIN.**'

'Charlie, what have we discovered causes you to change into an animal?'

Flora asked the question like Charlie was five years old.

'Stress,' answered Charlie.

'And what helps with stress? Think back to our meditation lessons with the mindfulness and yoga teacher. You remember the song she sang?'

'"I'm Too Sexy For My Shirt"?' suggested Wogan.

'No, Wogan. That wasn't it.'

'Oh. I don't know then,' Wogan said with a furrowed brow. 'It's so difficult!'

'Come on! You all know! The "Breath is Life" song!'

Mohsen, Charlie and Wogan looked at her blankly.

'Did none of you listen to her at all?'

Again they looked blankly at Flora.

Flora closed her eyes and began singing:

'Breathe in life!
Breathe in joy!
A deep breath is more blessed

Than a PlayStation toy!

Deep breath in!
Deep breath out!
Big breath out from your mouth
Suck it in up your snout!'

The song was met with a stony silence from the boys.

'That really doesn't ring ANY bells with you?'

The boys shrugged.

'I don't know why Miss Rainbow Gaia-Earthchild bothered, I really don't. You don't remember any of it? The body relaxing? The visualization techniques? Nothing?'

Mohsen, Wogan and Charlie looked blankly back at Flora.

'Honestly. Some people. Anyway, the point is deep breathing and imagining beautiful places and stuff relaxes you. Relaxing will stop you stressing. And hopefully – hopefully – that will stop you changing.'

Charlie had to admit it actually wasn't the worst plan he had ever heard. And right now, as it was their *only* plan, it was definitely their best plan.

And it was just a day later – just four days before the school play – that Flora's 'Miss Rainbow Gaia-Earthchild Relaxation Plan' was put to the test.

It was a hot sunny day, the sort of day when you couldn't walk barefoot outside because the pavement burned the soles of your feet, and Charlie was visiting his brother in hospital.

It was now three days away from his brother's big scan.

Charlie, sweat prickling underneath the collar of his shirt, was sitting on the edge of SmoothMove's bed waiting for him to reply.

SmoothMove was looking very serious, staring at the ceiling, hat on his bald head. After the longest time SmoothMove finally spoke.

'You promise you're totally telling the truth. Cross your heart?'

'Promise. Cross my heart,' Charlie replied.

'But that's unbelievable. Like properly amazing. I don't know what to say.'

'I know,' Charlie said.

'You've actually turned into a pigeon? And a snake? And a spider? That's just . . . I'm lost for words. You should be in the X-Men. My brother

is an actual, real-life superhero.'

'Well, I don't feel like a superhero,' Charlie said, but he couldn't help his heart swelling a little at his brother's words.

'You absolutely HAVE to keep it a secret, though. Don't tell anyone. Not even Mum or Dad,' SmoothMove said. 'Your life will be destroyed if people find out.'

'You sound just like Flora.'

'Sensible girl, that Flora. I've always said so,' SmoothMove said with the hint of a smile in his voice.

'No you haven't!' Charlie said. 'You've always said she's bonkers.'

SmoothMove laughed. 'OK! Maybe I got her wrong in the past. But anyway, you NEED to learn how to control it. Because if you can – then, wow, you really will be an actual superhero.'

'I'm trying,' said Charlie glumly. 'Flora has an idea actually.'

'Good. You should trust Flora.'

'You know those words have never, ever been spoken before by any human ever.'

Both Charlie and SmoothMove laughed at this. It felt good to see SmoothMove laugh, Charlie thought.

'So, how you feeling about the big scan then?' Charlie asked.

SmoothMove looked at Charlie, and another smile crossed his face.

'Piece of cake. No bother. It's definitely going to be fine. Get the all-clear and I'll be out of here.'

'Aren't you . . .' Charlie left the question hanging in the air.

'What? Scared? Give over. No way. Not a chance. Not half as scared as you will be when I get to play you at *FIFA* again. Then you'll know the meaning of scared. And destroyed. You'll know the meaning of that as well.'

Charlie wasn't sure that SmoothMove was telling the complete truth, but before he could say anything else their parents came in and it was time for him to go.

In a move that surprised them both Charlie jumped over and hugged SmoothMove.

'Get off me!' SmoothMove shouted. 'What do you think you're doing? Stop it! Ugh, now I'll have to speak to a doctor about getting a cure for a deadly case of Charlie Disease.'

Despite SmoothMove's words, though, Charlie had definitely felt the soft squeeze of a hug that his brother had given him in return.

★★★

Charlie was playing his Nintendo in his bedroom when it happened. The burning sun had made way for a swelteringly close late afternoon. All Charlie's windows were open, but there was no breeze. The soft clicking and snipping and digging sounds of his dad gardening drifted in on the still air. His dad had a portable radio outside that was playing soft classical music. It was a moment of stillness and peace.

All it took to break it were two words floating unwanted into Charlie's mind: *What if?*

What if SmoothMove's scan is bad news?

What if he's not getting better?

What if I never see him again?

The last thought came and the change started happening almost instantaneously. By now Charlie recognized the feelings in his body before they happened. It was like a faint warning alarm going off in the bottom of his mind. His heart beat faster. His stomach felt like it was plummeting down a deep trench to the bottom of an ocean. He knew it was coming.

He was changing again.

OK, quick, Charlie thought. *Relax! Breathe!*

He put the Nintendo down (being careful to save his game first).

He lay back on the floor, as Flora had instructed, and closed his eyes just as the electricity started shooting through him.

Breathe! thought Charlie. *Come on, breathe! Slowly! IN THROUGH THE MOUTH . . . OUT THROUGH THE NOSE . . .*

No, that was the wrong way round! *IN THROUGH THE NOSE . . . OUT THROUGH THE MOUTH . . .*

The electricity was surging through his body but it felt different this time. Slower. Like a dial that was only turned up to three or four instead of nine or ten.

He wasn't changing!

IN THROUGH THE NOSE . . . OUT THROUGH THE MOUTH . . .

He still wasn't changing! He'd done it! Charlie tried imagining he was lying on a beach,

breathing in calm, peaceful thoughts.

IN THROUGH THE NOSE . . . OUT THROUGH THE MOUTH . . .

The swelling electricity was still inside him, though. He could feel it and it wasn't going away.

Breathe. In. Out.

Was it growing?! Charlie suddenly felt like he was dangling over a precipice, hanging by a piece of thread. And then he felt it snap.

Noooo! Charlie panicked. He *was* changing! *Breathe!*

INTHROUGHTHENOSEOUT THROUGHTHEMOUTH . . .

INTHROUGHTHENOSEOUT THROUGHTHEMOUTH . . .

He could feel himself stretching. His body on fire.

INOUTINOUTINOUTINOUT OUT . . .

He was expanding, his skin toughening and turning grey. He was getting bigger, much bigger than Charlie. He was going to burst out of the room if he didn't stop growing soon. He could feel something immense growing out of his forehead.

Charlie knew what it was without looking.

And he knew what *he* was without looking.

The weight of his huge bulk made his floorboards creak. The thick grey leathery skin. The horn. Charlie plucked up the courage and tilted his head so he could see his faint reflection in the bedroom window. Even though he was prepared for what he was about to see, it still shocked him.

Charlie was a *rhino*.

He was a huge rhinoceros. In his not very large bedroom.

There was no way this was going to go well.

Unless he didn't do anything. Unless he could just wait it out.

I'd like to see Chairman Meow try to eat me this time, he thought.

Yes, waiting it out was the best and only way forward. Charlie's mum was out shopping and his dad was gardening, so the house would be empty for a while. If he could just

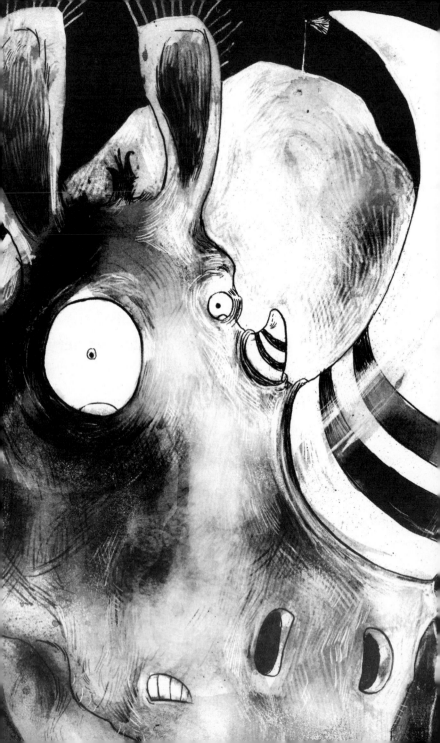

remain still, he might be OK. Might.

Charlie the rhinoceros stood motionless, breathing in and out of his flared nostrils.

And as he stood there a grim realization flashed across his rhino brain. Flora's plan had failed. He was back to square one. He couldn't control his power. He was going to change at the school play, he knew it, and that would be that. He'd be a science experiment for the rest of his life. The knowledge rolled around his stomach like a . . . like a . . .

Hang on a minute, Charlie thought. That wasn't knowledge rolling round his stomach. It was something much, much worse.

Oh no.

It couldn't be.

It could.

It was.

Charlie the rhinoceros needed a poo.

Now, why was this such a bad thing, you

might ask. What's so wrong with needing a poo? And that's a fair question. We all do sometimes. But what you have to understand is that an average rhinoceros can do quite a lot of poo. It can actually do as much as twenty kilograms a day, which is a LOT. The average six-year-old child weighs twenty kilograms. A poo the size and weight of a six-year-old child laid by a majestic rhino gallivanting across the vast open plains of Africa is one thing. However, a poo the size and weight of a six-year-old child laid in an average-size bedroom is a VERY different proposition. Just imagine for a moment the sight of that ENORMOMASSIVE poo lying on your own bedroom carpet. The smell of it. The stain it would leave. There would be no hiding it from his parents, Charlie thought. How on earth would he explain to them the sudden appearance of a steaming poo the size of nine Yorkshire terriers?

He couldn't.

He had to think fast.

And then inspiration hit him, like a massive rhino poo hitting the floor.

In front of him was an open window. If he was able to turn round, and if he was able to position his huge rhino bum perfectly, then he could poo straight out the window. It was a pretty desperate plan, but it was the only one he had.

Slowly, ever so slowly, Rhino-Charlie started edging round, his horn tearing his football posters and scraping a great gouge in the wallpaper underneath. He'd be in deep trouble for that later. *Forget about it for now*, Charlie thought. He had bigger things to worry about, namely the blast that he could feel was about to erupt out of his colossal rhino bum at any moment.

Despite the imminent explosive rhino poo Charlie still had to be super-careful. Round he slowly turned, his huge hooves crushing toys and books and comics as he went. Fortunately his Nintendo was on his bed, so was saved a rhino-crushing. His bum was pointed directly over his bed now, though, and if he didn't move quickly, his Nintendo (and the whole of his bed) would get covered in a massive mound of poo.

He tried turning round a little faster. His immense grey bum knocked over his bedside table, sending a lamp, a glass of water and a Bluetooth speaker to the floor.

And then, finally, his bum was in front of the window.

Charlie edged backwards until he felt his bum touch the window frame. If he went any further, he'd knock the window completely out. He could feel the late-summer sunshine on his backside, so he must be in approximately the right place.

Charlie lifted his tail.

And it was just in the nick of time.

Out from Charlie's bum shot a poo so fast and so massive it could have filled a bath in three seconds flat. It flew through the window, arcing perfectly towards the ground, and Charlie let out a sigh of relief.

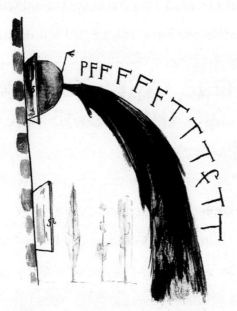

The feeling only lasted about half a second, though, before a wail from the garden ripped through the summer evening.

'WHAT THE . . .?!'

Charlie knew straight away what had happened.

It was his father screaming and shouting.

His father who had been gardening.

Gardening just below Charlie's window.

Charlie couldn't help it. He started laughing. But as he was still a rhino it sounded like a rough snuffle of delight.

'WHERE THE FLIBBERING HECK DID THIS COME FROM?!'

Charlie's father yelled.

Charlie felt bubbles of laughter ripple through him.

And then, out of nowhere, he felt the change come quick and fast. He was shrinking. His horn was disappearing. His skin softening. His fingers growing, hair returning.

Before he knew it he was Charlie again.

He rushed to the open window, fearing what he was about to see.

It was worse than he had possibly imagined.

There, directly underneath the window, still holding his spade, was Charlie's dad. Two eyes blinked up at Charlie from a face completely covered in rhino poo. A few flies were hovering around his dad as he stood there in shock, open-mouthed.

'IT . . . IT JUST FELL . . . OUT OF THE SKY . . .' Charlie's dad stammered. 'OUT OF NOWHERE . . . ALL THIS . . . POO . . . ON TO MY HEAD.'

Charlie couldn't help bursting into laughter.

'IT'S NOT FUNNY, CHARLIE! I'M COMPLETELY COVERED!' his dad shouted up at him.

Charlie roared laughing, tears streaming down his face.

'GO AND GET THE HOSE, CHARLIE!'

Charlie couldn't move for laughing.

'GET THE BLASTED HOSE, CHARLIE! OH GOD, THERE'S SO MANY FLIES! QUICKLY, CHARLIE!'

A few moments later, as he hosed his poo-plastered father down while he muttered about how 'a plane must have emptied its blasted toilet in mid-air', and as the summer sun gently slid behind the trees that backed on to their house, Charlie realized he hadn't laughed so hard for a long, long time.

CHAPTER 13

The day of the play had finally arrived and there was a buzz of anticipation outside the school, with parents, pupils and teachers all chattering excitedly. But not for Charlie, Mohsen, Wogan and Flora, who had agreed to meet outside to wish Charlie good luck. A black cloud had been hanging over the friends for days.

Wogan looked up at the sky.

'I really wish that black cloud would go away. It's just been hanging over us. For days.'

'Yes,' agreed Mohsen. 'It's like it's a . . . metaphor for something. But I can't think what,' he said glumly.

'My impending and certain doom?' suggested Charlie.

'Ohhhhhh yeaaahh.' Mohsen nodded, grinning widely at the new-found connection in his brain. 'That must be it. Charlie's impending and certain doom.'

'It's not certain,' muttered Flora, who was sitting on the ground, eyes closed and brow furrowed, her fingers church-steepled at her chin.

Charlie, Mohsen and Wogan turned to Flora.

'What do you mean?' asked Mohsen.

'I mean it's not certain. Charlie's doom,' Flora replied, not moving a muscle.

'How can it not be certain?' Charlie asked, temper rising in his voice. 'Since this whole thing started, every time I've got stressed I've changed into an animal. Every. Single. Time.'

Flora opened her eyes and looked seriously at Charlie, but waited for him to continue.

'What makes you think that *this* time,' Charlie said, his face beginning to turn red, 'when I have to sing a STUPID song about a *sad potato* in front of the WHOLE SCHOOL, is going to be ANY different? It's going to be WORSE and I'm going to change into who knows what – probably something *totally* embarrassing like a gnu or a naked mole rat – and I'm going to be sent away to some science lab for the rest of my life. That's it. I'm done for. Game over.'

Charlie finished his rant, and glared at Flora, daring her to reply. Flora looked back, meeting Charlie's stare.

'Those black clouds are really, really thick now,' Wogan said, peering at the sky. 'It looks like it's about to absolutely tip it down.'

'It's not going to rain. And Charlie won't necessarily change,' Flora replied simply.

'Gah! What do you know?'

'Firstly, Charlie, I know you need to stop thinking like that. If you keep convincing yourself you're going to change, then you're just going to make yourself more and more stressed and then you definitely WILL change.'

'Oh, great, thanks for telling me – that'll help. Now it's my fault.'

'I'm not saying it's your fault,' Flora said calmly. 'I'm saying you have the power to change things. Bad things happen, Charlie. Accept them. It's not what happens to you in life – it's how you deal with it that sets out the person you are. You're the bravest person I know, Charlie McGuffin, and whatever happens you'll deal with it. You're my best friend, and if you change in front of the school and the scientists come to take you away, then me and Mohsen and Wogan will do everything we can to protect you. Whatever it takes.'

Mohsen and Wogan both nodded their

heads vigorously.

Charlie swallowed. And blinked quickly. He wanted to reply to Flora, but found he had quite lost his voice.

'Anyway,' said Flora, 'we now know something else about your situation from what you've told us about the rhino incident.'

'If you're going to poo out of a window, check that your dad isn't pruning the roses just below?' suggested Mohsen.

'That's true,' said Flora. 'But that's not what I'm getting at. I'm talking about laughter. Once you started laughing, Charlie, you changed back immediately.'

'Oh yeah . . .' said Charlie.

'So,' continued Flora, business-like. 'We therefore know the following:

1. You turn into an animal when you get stressed.

2. Deep-breathing and relaxing helps to

slow it down, but it doesn't stop it.

3. Happiness changes you back.

'Now, that might not be the complete answer to everything that's going on, but it's an awful lot more than we knew when you first started changing. We are close to a cure, Charlie. So close.'

Mr O'Dere, the Irish caretaker, started ringing a handbell, barking at everybody to start taking their seats. The four friends walked back towards their classroom to get ready for the play, all of them lost in thought about Charlie's problem (apart from Wogan, who was wondering if a naked mole rat was a real animal or not). Behind them, unnoticed, a split appeared in the black clouds overhead, and a shaft of golden sunlight broke through.

★★★

They may have been closer to the cure, but it still felt like a million miles away to Charlie.

He had watched with dread through the curtains as the hall had filled up with parents and children until almost every seat was taken, apart from some in the front few rows. Now, pale-faced, he was stood backstage, all dressed up in his potato outfit, heart pounding in his mouth. Good-luck wishes from Flora and Mohsen still rang in his ears. Wogan was already on stage. Charlie could hear him with Cara.

In a matter of minutes he would have to go on himself.

'You're going to change,' came a sudden whisper in Charlie's ear. It was Dylan, looking

painfully smug in his carrot costume. 'And don't think you're going to get away with it this time, McGuffin. I'm going to make sure everyone sees. There's nothing you can do to stop me.'

Charlie found he had nothing smart to say back to Dylan. He was right.

'Well, what do you want from me, Dylan?

You expect me to go bananas or cry or punch you?'

'No, Mr McGuffin, I expect you to change!'

'Oh God, you are just so completely insane.'

'The distance between insanity and genius is measured only by success,' Dylan replied, eyes ablaze.

'Hang on,' said Charlie in disbelief. 'Are you quoting James Bond villains at me?'

'Goodbye, Mr McGuffin.'

And with that Dylan turned around and walked away.

It was time.

★★★

Flora and Mohsen sat in the audience biting their fingernails.[17] Neither dared breathe as they waited for Charlie to come out on stage for his big song.

---

[17] Their own fingernails, not each other's.

And then, out of the corner of her eye, Flora saw somebody slipping into a seat near the front of the audience.

Somebody she wasn't expecting to see.

Somebody Charlie *really* wasn't expecting to see.

And it gave her a brilliant idea . . .

★★★

Charlie closed his eyes for a moment, steeling himself.

And then he stood up, and walked into the wings.

It was dark and, just before he stepped on the stage, he felt a tap on his shoulder. It was Dylan.

Grinning his smug grin, he produced a key from beneath his carrot costume with a dramatic flourish and waved it in front of Charlie's face, and then locked the door they had just walked through. Then, with a final even smugger grin, he walked out on to the stage.

Dylan had locked the door. Charlie's only exit was blocked. If he started changing on stage now, he couldn't just escape through the wings. He'd have to try to run all the way through the audience. With a heavy sinking feeling Charlie realized that Dylan had destroyed his one chance of escape.

Charlie trudged out on to the stage, where Dylan was waiting for him expectantly.

It was hot and bright. Two spotlights were shining on to the stage: one trained directly on Dylan, one on Charlie.

Charlie blinked in the glare. It was so bright he couldn't see out into the audience. It was a sea of black behind the light. But he could feel them waiting: rustling, hushed.

Trickles of sweat were running down his

forehead and back. His palms were wet. He was already feeling dizzy. Dylan, a victorious look on his face, turned to Charlie, looked him in the eye and mouthed one word:

Change.

And then Dylan started singing. A carrot had never sounded happier.

Straight away it started. Charlie's heart began to beat faster and his stomach plummeted.

His eye began to twitch.

Then his other eye began to twitch.

Before Dylan was halfway through his song Charlie could feel fire racing through his body, his nerves searing with electricity.

This was it.

He was changing in front of the whole school.

★★★

Even from where she was sitting in the audience

Flora could see Charlie's eyes glaze over with fear.

Deep down in the pit of her stomach she knew it was all about to go terribly, terribly wrong.

She knew Charlie was changing.

And she knew exactly what she needed to do.

She jumped out of her seat and began pushing past people, running towards the back of the hall.

Colm Flower, the beefy Year Six captain of the school rugby team, was manning Charlie's spotlight. He looked up in surprise as Flora appeared by his side.

'Whadda you want?' he asked

'I need to borrow that spotlight for a minute,' she said, smiling sweetly.

'Bog off,' replied Colm.

'Now that's not very polite,' replied Flora. 'I'll give you till a count of three. One . . . two . . .'

★★★

Dylan was reaching the end of his song.

Charlie's body was fizzing, explosions of electricity inside him.

It was happening.

Breathe, Charlie told himself. *Breathe!*

Charlie tried taking slow, deep breaths, calming himself. In, out. In, out.

But although the fire and the electricity racing through his veins was slowing it wasn't stopping.

Dylan finished his song and took a bow.

The audience applauded.

Silence fell, everybody waiting for Charlie to sing.

Seconds felt like years.

Then Charlie felt his body change.

The insides of his body squeezing.

Underneath his costume his body started to itch, hair sprouting on his legs. On his back. On his stomach.

His face.

This was it. It was all over . . .

'Three!'

There was a yell of pain and a sudden

clattering sound from the back of the hall and the spotlight swung off Charlie, plunging him into darkness.

Charlie's arms were lengthening; he could reach the stage floor with them. Charlie knew no one could see him now, but that wouldn't last. When the spotlight swung back on to him the whole world would know he was a freak.

But the spotlight didn't come back to him. Instead, it arced into the audience, strafing the front few rows until it landed on one person.

A boy a bit older than Charlie, wearing a hat to cover his baldness.

Charlie couldn't believe what he was seeing.

It was impossible.

There, sat between Charlie's mum and dad, was SmoothMove.

And Charlie knew that could only mean one thing: the scan was good. His big brother didn't need that operation after all. He was coming home.

Charlie felt his heart burst with joy and relief and, as those happy feelings flooded through him, he immediately felt himself changing again. Changing back to who he should be: a small nine-year-old boy standing awkwardly on stage in a potato costume in a strange school play about vegetables in love.

And at the very moment Charlie felt he was completely back to normal the spotlight swung back on to him.

Next to Charlie, looking utterly furious, Dylan glared at him.

Charlie winked at Dylan, then closed his eyes and took a deep breath.

And then Charlie sang, with happiness bursting out of every fibre of his body and with a smile plastered across his face, a song about a sad potato.

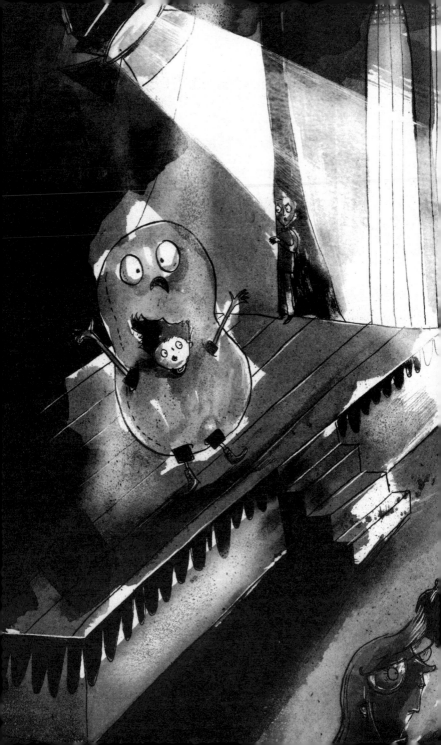

And that's that, there or thereabouts. There are a few things to wrap up, and then there will be time for questions.

Ms Fyre and Mr Wind were 'disappointed' with Charlie for 'grinning like a loon' all the way through his song. Charlie grinned all the way through his telling-off too, at which point Mr Wind and Ms Fyre began to worry Charlie had a screw loose. In fact, Mr Wind and Ms Fyre were *so* disappointed they immediately had to go off to a local wine bar together, to discuss what went wrong with the play and how it could be improved next year.

Dylan remained furious with Charlie for a long time. He had been the only one to see Charlie change into a chimpanzee, and the only one to see him change back. His plans had come to nothing. But he would spend many days, weeks and months planning and plotting how he could expose Charlie to the wider world for the freak that he was.

Mohsen and Wogan remained in awe of Flora. They also remained slightly terrified of Flora. No one knew exactly what Flora had said or done to Colm Flower in order to gain control of the spotlight on the night of the play, but he now ran the other way down the corridor whenever he saw her coming.

Flora stayed exactly the same. And so she should because she's AWESOME.

The McGuffins were a family, together again. SmoothMove was back home and, although it took some time, he got completely better. It didn't take any time at all for him to beat Charlie at *FIFA*, though.

And Charlie? He had his brother back. And he never changed into an animal again. Well, not for a while at least.

THE END

So, there you go. That's it. The end. The finish line. I hope you enjoyed reading it as much as I enjoyed writing it. A lot more actually, because to be honest, writing it was a pretty dreadful experience. My fingers *still* have blisters.

So. Questions?

Q: Charlie, nine years old, asks: *'My name is Charlie and I am also nine years old. Is this book about me?'*

A: Do you turn into animals, Charlie? No? Exactly. Well, the book isn't about you then. Obviously.

Q: Josh, nine, from Whitstable asks: *'If this book was so miserable to write, why did you bother doing it? And it's not even a particularly long book. It's only just over 27,500 words. That's not long for a book. The Harry Potter series is over a million words. That's over thirty-five times as long as your book.'*

A: Oh, marvellous, it's Josh from Whitstable again. Didn't you ask enough questions last time? Well, to answer your question, yes, the Harry Potter series is forty times longer than this book, but you know what? It's not the quantity of words that matters. It's the *quality*. And I like to think that one word in this book is equal to about forty words from J. K. Rowling waffling on about Professor Bumblebore and Severus Snooze, right? RIGHT?

Q: Bethany, aged two, from A Couple of Houses Down the Road asks: *'Why did you* *have to make Dylan so mean?'*

A: Let me tell you something, Bethany: I didn't make Dylan mean. Life made him mean. Dylan has had a tough time and, deep down, he's really unhappy. And most angry or unpleasant people are almost always, deep down, very unhappy.

Q: **Emily, ten, from Frimpton-on-Sea asks:** *'Is there a deeper meaning to this book? Exactly what important message are you trying to give the reader? Because if you don't have a deeper meaning, then is this just a silly story about a boy who turns into animals?'*

A: Thank you for the question, Emily.

Q: **Emily, ten, from Frimpton-on-Sea asks:** *'Are you trying to avoid the question? You DO have a deep and important message behind the book, don't you?'*

A: Of course I'm not avoiding the question.

And of COURSE I have a deep message in the book. And the message is . . . the message is . . . Ooh! Look! Behind you! There's a big flying thing! Oh, you just missed it. It's gone now. Never mind. Anyway, what were we talking about? Next question, please.

Q: **Nathaniella Warglefloom, sixty-seven, from Banjax-on-Thames asks:** *'I noticed that a previous questioner, "Bethany", was only two years old. That can't be right. Are you just making all these people up? Are the questions even real?'*
A: What *is* real, Nathaniella? Are you real? Am *I* real? Does it actually matter what's real and what isn't?

Q: **Charlie, nine years old, asks:** *'You actually didn't let me answer your question. You just answered for me. In answer to your question,* *yes, actually, I do turn into animals. And my surname is McGuffin. And my best friends are Wogan, Mohsen and Flora. This book is clearly based on my life. And I did not give you permission to turn my life story into a poorly written book. I have sought legal advice and I will see you in court.'*

A: This is a question-and-answer session, Charlie. You just gave a series of statements there and no question. And I have ALSO sought legal advice. Unfortunately they have told me to stop writing immediately. There would have been loads more in this book, loads of stuff that would have been way better. But I am now not allowed to write any more. Big shame. You've spoiled everybody's fun, Charlie McGuffin. I hope you're happy.

Puffin Books

80 Strand

London

Dear Reader,

Many of you have written to our esteemed
company to complain about the lack of chickens
in this story. You were explicitly promised by
the 'author', on the very cover of this 'book',
that the central character would turn into a
chicken. We are saddened to report that the
author lied to you. He drew you in with promises
of chickens and then betrayed your trust. That
is unforgivable.

We were similarly taken in by the author's
deceit. We published this book in good faith,
and the lack of chickens has come as a shock and
disappointment to us too. We can only apologize

to you, our valued readers, and assure you that this situation will not arise again. The editor responsible for checking chicken-inclusions has been dismissed, and we have agreed that *all* future books published by our company shall include at least one chicken.

Some of our forthcoming chicken-featured publications include: *Lord of the Wings*, *Moby Chick*, *The Adventures of Cluckleberry Finn,* and *Great Eggspectations* by Charles Chickens.

Needless to say, we shall not be working with the author again. He is a disreputable liar and a writer of little talent. We recommend that you never read any more of his tawdry tales.

With deepest respect and humble apologies,
Yours faithfully,

The Publisher

Read on for
a sneak peek
of Charlie's
next adventure!

CHAPTER 1

Charlie McGuffin was being followed.

A malevolent shadow was watching him. Waiting.

Something – or someone – was stalking him through the corridors of the school. A dark presence, menacing, unseen and unknowable –

'Look, Dylan, I know it's you following me. I can see you there,' Charlie said, hands on hips. 'Can you actually stop? You just look weird doing it. Seriously, Dylan – come out from behind the pillar.'

Dylan stepped out from behind a pillar.

'And take that ridiculous hat off,' Charlie added.

Dylan took off the ridiculous hat, a floppy summer hat borrowed from his mum.

'And the sunglasses. Take those off as well.'

Dylan took off the sunglasses.

'Now *please* stop following me.'

Dylan stepped forward, chest puffed. 'You know you can run, McGuffin, but you can't hide. You. Can't. Hide.' A smile slid across Dylan's face like a slug trail. 'I'm your shadow. Your dark half. Wherever you go, I will be there. Hunting you. Ready to pounce like a . . . like a . . . frog.'

'A frog? A pouncing frog? Frogs don't even pounce.'

'Yes, they do. They pounce on flies. And you're my fly. Trapped in my web.'

'A . . . frog web?' said Charlie, looking a little baffled.

'You think you're so clever, McGuffin, don't you? Well, you're not. Your silly little friends might think you're a genius –'

'I'm not sure they do actually. In fact, I'm pretty certain Flora thinks I'm the total opposite. She even said that to me yesterday. She said "Charlie, you are actually the total opposite of a genius."'

'Enough!' Dylan held his hand up. 'Just know that I am going to capture you.' Dylan opened his hand. Inside was a matchbox. He shook it. It was empty. 'I am going to wait until you change into an animal. And I'm going to trap you. And then you won't be laughing. Or if you are, no one will hear you. Because you'll be trapped in a matchbox. A matchbox prison!'

Dylan started laughing to himself and then walked off, still laughing wildly, leaving Charlie standing alone in an empty corridor.

Charlie couldn't help it – Dylan was getting to him. He could feel his stress levels begin to rise, little shivers of electricity darting through him. This was the first sign that Charlie was about to change. He closed his eyes and breathed deeply a couple of times, focusing on his breath. Then he opened his eyes wide.

'Hey, Dylan!' Charlie shouted to the small figure at the end of the long corridor. 'Dylan! I think I'm changing! Quick!'

Dylan turned round and began running back as fast as he could.

'Quick, Dylan! It's happening!'

Dylan sprinted as fast as he could. He reached Charlie, panting.

'Oh, sorry,' Charlie said. 'False alarm.'

Dylan glared at Charlie. 'WHAT?'

'I'm sorry!' Charlie said, grinning. 'I could have sworn I started feeling it. Ah, well, it's an unpredictable science, this whole changing business. Better luck next time. Actually there won't be a next time. You're wasting your time. I've worked out how to control it, you see, so I can absolutely guarantee a hundred per cent that there'll be no more Charlie changing into *anything*.'

Charlie winked at Dylan, and then walked off, laughing maniacally, leaving Dylan stood alone in the empty corridor.

AUTHOR'S NOTE

If you haven't read Book 1 in this series, *Charlie Changes Into a Chicken*, then you're probably pretty confused about what's going on right now.

Tough luck.

You should have bought Book 1.

You come waltzing in here thinking, *Oh, I don't need to read Book 1. I'm very clever and I'm sure I'll work out what's happening as I go along.*

Well, NOW who looks silly? You haven't a clue what's going on, have you? You don't know who Charlie is or who Dylan is or why Dylan is trying to put Charlie in a matchbox. All I can say is good luck with the rest of the book, pinheads.

AUTHOR'S NOTE II

The publishers have informed me that apparently I am not allowed to refer to my 'valued readers' as 'pinheads'. They have therefore instructed me to apologize to you. So, here we are:

I'm really, really, truly sorry.[1]

I hope you're happy.[2]

They have also instructed me to give you a quick rundown on what happens in Book 1. So, for those of you too lazy to go to the library to get it, here we go:

Charlie McGuffin keeps turning into animals. He discovers, with the help of his friends Flora, Mohsen and Wogan, that he changes when he is stressed and upset. Together

[1] I'm not really sorry. I lied. Pinheads.

[2] I don't.

they work out that he can control it (sort of) if he relaxes and tries to be happy. Also, Charlie's nemesis, Dylan, who you just met, saw Charlie change and basically went very weird and turned into a bit of a movie villain who's determined to expose Charlie's secret to the whole world.

OK, now you've caught up, shall we get on with the story? Good.

CHAPTER 1 (CONTINUED)

'Wow! So you're sure you have the whole changing-into-an-animal thing under control?' asked Mohsen.

'Oh yes. Absolutely,' replied Charlie.

It was playtime, but he was sitting with Flora and Mohsen in a noisy classroom, as cold sleety rain was pattering against the window. Flora was absent-mindedly flicking through a magazine called *The World's Fluffiest But Deadly Animals*. The autumn term was coming to an end, and Christmas was on everybody's mind.

The class had spent the morning making paper chains, and they were now hung all across the classroom.

Wogan was over the other side of the room, talking to the new girl Daisy. Daisy had long brown curly hair and she loved unicorns more than anything. And ponies. But mostly unicorns. Wogan had spent the whole of the past couple of days telling anybody who listened that he absolutely did *not* think Daisy was pretty and that he had, in fact, actually *always* thought unicorns were 'cool'.

'You're totally sure?' Flora said to Charlie, eyeing him suspiciously.

'Yes! Definitely. Sheesh! I told you. Dylan tried getting me to change in the corridor just now, but I stopped it. So I'm completely one hundred per cent sure that I am totally in control of the whole changing-into-an-animal thing and it won't happen again. I can guarantee that.'

Charlie couldn't guarantee that.

In fact, Charlie, deep down, wasn't at all sure that he had control of the whole changing-into-an-animal thing. But he wanted to be brave in front of Flora, who had managed to increase in awesomeness by about six per cent since Book 1 after winning the Interschool County Rap Battle with her rap 'Top Flor'.

'Charlie, you don't have to be brave in front of me, you know. You can tell me the truth,' Flora said, placing a hand on Charlie's shoulder.

'Will you stop putting that thing on me?' Charlie said, knocking the fake toy hand off his shoulder. 'Honestly, it's just weird.'

'Well, it's just . . . It's just . . . It's a big thing to have to learn and it might take time to get the hang of it completely,' said Flora, picking up her toy hand and putting it in her bag. 'Don't be disappointed if you do change again.'

Charlie made a humphing noise.

Wogan wandered over. 'Hey, Charlie,' said Wogan. 'Have you changed into any animals again?'

'NO! I HAVE NOT! I CAN CONTROL IT, OK?' Charlie snapped.

Mohsen and Wogan edged away from Charlie.

'O-K,' said Wogan, holding his hands up. 'That's great. Good for you.'

'Guys!' whispered Flora. 'Keep it down! We

don't want everyone to hear!'

'It really is quite amazing,' said Mohsen in a low voice, 'that you, a small boy of just nine years of age, have succeeded so easily in totally mastering your mysterious and extraordinary power, the likes of which mankind has never seen before.'

Charlie narrowed his eyes. 'You don't believe me! You don't think I have mastered it! Well, I have. It won't happen again,' said Charlie certainly.

***

Well, thought Charlie later that very evening, as he began licking himself clean, *I was certainly wrong*.

And why was Charlie licking himself clean?

Well, to find that out let's go back a short while in time . . .

Charlie had arrived home feeling pretty chipper. It had been a good day: his class had had the supply teacher in all day, because their usual teacher Arthur Wind was on a three-day intensive strategy course with the headteacher, Miss Fyre, on a boat on the Norfolk Broads.

Mr Pointment, the supply teacher, had let them sit wherever they liked, *and* had let them do whatever they wanted in class as long as they were *very* quiet and hadn't bothered him. He had sat at the front of the class for almost the whole day, eyes closed and holding his head in his hands, apart from a couple of times when he'd suddenly run out of the room, a look of pale urgency on his face.

Charlie's good mood was spoilt not long after he got home. He and SmoothMove (Charlie's big brother who had been ill but was now much better) had wolfed down their tea and were lying in front of the TV under the glow of the

Christmas-tree lights, playing *FIFA 19*.

Charlie was losing as per usual.

They heard the key in the front door. It was their dad, home unusually early. He didn't poke his head into the sitting room to say hello, which was also unusual.

Charlie and SmoothMove could hear a low muttered conversation between their mum and dad coming from the kitchen. They could tell by the tone of their parents' voices that all wasn't right. SmoothMove and Charlie looked at each.

'What's that all about?' asked Charlie.

'Dunno,' SmoothMove replied. 'Boring adult stuff, I reckon.' He shrugged, then turned back to the game, but a nervous tension still rippled between them.

A little while later, their mum called them both into the kitchen. They both wandered in. Their mum and dad were sat at the table, both looking serious, both with their arms crossed.

'Could you sit down?' Charlie's dad said. 'We need to have a family conference.'

Charlie knew a family conference meant something big. Either something good-big or something bad-big. Unless Charlie was very much mistaken, the looks on his parents' faces said this was something bad-big. His first thought was something was wrong with SmoothMove again, but his brother was sitting next to him looking healthy and equally mystified at his dad's behaviour, so it couldn't be *that*.

'I'm afraid to say,' his dad announced, 'we're going to have to tighten our belts a little for a while.'

'Why? Are we losing weight?' Charlie asked.

'No, Charlie. It's a phrase. It means we are going to have to save some money. A lot of money actually.'

This sounded like pretty terrible news to Charlie, especially as Christmas was fast approaching.

'You see,' continued his dad. 'There's been a bit of trouble at work and it could have some pretty serious repercussions.'

Charlie thought that Reaper Cushions sounded both awesome and comfortable but knew, by looking at his dad's face, that now was not the time to say that.

'What sort of repercussions, Dad?' SmoothMove asked.

'Well, it looks like we might have to downsize.'

'Downsize? How do you mean?' Charlie asked.

'I mean that we might have to sell the house,' his father replied.

Silence hit the kitchen. Charlie stared at his dad.

'And then what?' asked SmoothMove. 'Where will we live?'

'Well, there's a chance we might have to move in with Aunt Brenda. Just for a short while. Until we sort things out more permanently.'

'Aunt Brenda?!' cried Charlie. 'We can't move in with Aunt Brenda!'

Aunt Brenda's house was all the way over the other side of town and it smelled of cat wee. Aunt Brenda had seventeen cats and one leg. She refused to get a fancy modern prosthetic leg, and as she walked around her house her wooden leg rapped on the floorboards like the deck of a pirate ship.

'Now, it's not certain,' his dad continued. 'Nothing's set in stone. Fingers crossed, we'll be able to sort out the work issue and everything will just go back to normal. But in the meantime we're going to have to make a few savings.' Charlie's dad gave the table a watery smile.

'But try not to worry, kids. We'll all pull together as a family,' said Charlie's mum. 'And if the worst comes to the worst, we can sell one of you,' she continued with a twinkle in her eye.

'Oh, that's a good idea!' said Dad, a cheeky smile crinkling his face. 'That would be a proper money-saver. But it will be too tough to decide which one of you to keep, so you boys need to do rock-paper-scissors and the loser gets eBayed.'

They all laughed, breaking the tension a little.

But although his dad might have been smiling again, Charlie couldn't mistake the shadow of concern still clouding his father's eyes. And that shadow gave Charlie a knot in his stomach.